Soldier Daddy a DDlg Military Romance

K CARTY

Copyright © 2023 K Carty

This is based on a true story. I have tried to recreate events, locales, and conversations from my personal memories of them. For privacy reasons, some potentially identifying details such as names, locations, occupations, and dates may have been changed.

No part of this book may be reproduced, or stored in a retrieval system, or transmitted in any form or by any means, electronic, mechanical, photocopying, recording, or otherwise, without express written permission of the publisher.

All rights reserved.

ISBN: 979-8-9892927-7-6

DEDICATION

To my husband. I love you, A&F.

CONTENTS

	Acknowledgments	i
1	ORDERS	1
2	FAMILY FUN OR FAMILY FAIL?	Pg 6
3	NEVER GOODBYE, ONLY LATERS	Pg 18
4	ONLY 364-ISH DAYS LEFT, RIGHT?	Pg 24
5	IT'S LIKE GROUNDHOG DAY, UNTIL IT'S NOT	Pg 29
6	FINALLY, SOMETHING TO LOOK FORWARD TO	Pg 36
7	CAN WE BE KINKY?	Pg 40
8	FEELING SEXY AND…	Pg 46
9	AND THEN THERE WAS CHANGE	Pg 53
10	IT'S ALL FALLING APART	Pg 67
11	AND TIME GOES ON AND ON (AND ON)	Pg 73
12	A (CHOKED) BREATH OF FRESH AIR	Pg 80

13	THE SPICE IS STILL SPICY (AND THEN SOME)	Pg 88
14	ANNIVERSARY TRIP MIDDLESPACE	Pg 98
15	WATER PARK BEFORE THE WATER WORKS	Pg 106
16	THE TIME HAS COME, THE WIFEY SAID, TO TALK OF DEPRESSING THINGS: OF PLANE RIDES, AND SICK KIDS, OF MURPHY'S LAW AND THINGs	Pg 117
17	TRY, TRY AGAIN	Pg 127
18	IMPOSTER	Pg 132
19	"I HATE IT HERE"	Pg 137
20	IT'S HOMECOMING DAY!	Pg 146
EPI	EPILOGUE	Pg 152
	NOTE FROM THE AUTHOR	
	ABOUT	

ACKNOWLEDGMENTS

This book likely will not be like many DDlg or Military romances on the market. This is a story of resilience, exploration, and growth. Remember, kink is customizable, and all dynamics are different. This book has inspiration from my real life as a seasoned military spouse and how my marriage has grown and changed, however, many themes are very much fictional.

1
ORDERS

SARAH

"I leave in two days, babe."

I step into our bedroom, away from our two little girls as I process the information my husband, Ryan, just dropped on me. "No-notice deployments usually give at least 72 hours before wheels up," I point out. I know from experience. While I was on active duty, I was called off leave to deploy on a no-notice tasking. That mission changed my life. It's where I met Ryan.

"This is different, babe. My connecting flight is on Friday. I'm leaving here Thursday, so I don't miss it." It's Tuesday afternoon. That's not even two full days. It's times like these I really hate his job.

"Okay. I'll start working on things here. What

are we going to tell the girls?"

"We'll figure it out. I'll be home soon. Can you order a pizza? We'll have some family time."

"Yeah. I don't feel like cooking now anyway. I love you."

"Love you, too, babe. Laters."

Ryan disconnects from the call, and I flop on my bed to cry into my pillow. I need a few minutes before I can function. I give myself maybe five minutes of self-pity before I get to work. I grab socks, underwear, uniform t-shirts, and some comfy civilian clothes for Ryan to wear off duty. I debate whether to include his physical training uniforms or not. The units overseas don't always have time to do PT together and often work out individually on their own time. He can figure out the PT uniform stuff when he gets home.

Once I've gathered everything I can immediately think of, I start a load of laundry and plop down on the couch next to my girls as they watch Octonauts. This has become a favorite of my youngest's since quarantine for COVID-19 started earlier this year. I open the web browser on my phone and order pizza for dinner. Not that I have much of an appetite, but the kids will need to eat. The pizza won't take long to get here, and I haven't heard from Ryan in a while.

ME: Pizza should be here in 30-45 minutes. You done yet?
RYAN: Almost

ME: What does "Almost" mean? Do you have an ETA?
RYAN: I'm working on it, babe. I'll be there as soon as I can.

It's difficult to read tone through text messages, but I know he's holding back irritation. After seven years of marriage, you learn a few things about your partner. I don't mean to nag him, but we're losing precious time together. And we still need to tell the kids.

Ryan arrives home moments before the pizza delivery driver rings the doorbell.

"Grab the dog," I call out. Callie, our six-year-old, grabs the dog's collar so I can answer the door without her running off. I sign the delivery receipt for the pizza and carry the boxes to the dining room. Callie releases the dog. "Becca, feed the dog. Callie get plates and drinks, please."

"I'm starving," Ryan says as he walks out of our bedroom. "I didn't eat lunch today."

"Well, I ordered plenty. And the brownie thing, too." Ryan gives me his 'Of course you did' look and smirks at me. "What? I'm in a shitty mood. I wanted something yummy."

"You're good, babe." He pulls me in for a huge hug and kisses me on top of my head. I hold back tears. The kids don't know yet. I don't want them to see me cry.

RYAN

She's pissed. I can't say I blame her. It's not that this tasking was a surprise. We've known for months now, but the last-minute notice of my leaving **is** a surprise.

This won't be the first time I've gone away to support the Army. I've served overseas on a few different missions, but this will be our longest apart, and the longest I will be away from my girls. Rebecca is only three and Callie is six. I've missed so much of Rebecca's life already. Short overseas missions, field exercises, and professional military training...I've been gone for what feels like most of her short life. All I can do is make the most of the next few days.

"I think we should keep the kids home from daycare for the next couple of days. I want to spend every moment I can with you all. Can you call out of work?" I quietly ask my wife, hoping the girls don't overhear. We'll tell them tomorrow.

"I don't think Terry will have a problem with it. I'll text him and let him know what's going on." Sarah sends the text and sets her phone to the side. She's so sad now, and nothing I say or do will change it. This is our reality until I can retire from the Army, and we still have about seven years before that's possible. Sarah's phone lights up with a notification. She picks it up to check the alerts. "Terry says I'm good to go and to take all the time I need."

We finish the episode of Octonauts and turn on Frozen. It's one of Sarah's favorite movies and the kids enjoy it as well. My wife deserves all the comfort she can get, especially in the months to come. I reach across the center console of our loveseat and grasp her hand in mine, intertwining our fingers. I bring her hand to my mouth and kiss her. She looks and me and gives me a sad smile. This is going to be much harder than I thought.

After two hours of watching my wife lip-sync through the entire movie, being especially charismatic during Olaf's number, the torture has ended, and we call it a night. We made the mistake of telling the girls they would be staying home tomorrow and now they think they get to stay up late. That's a 'No'.

"We'll do something fun tomorrow, but if you don't go to sleep, you will be too tired for Family Fun Day," Sarah says, kissing the children 'Goodnight'.

"Stay in bed or we won't go anywhere tomorrow," I warn, turning out the light and pulling the door closed.

"Yes, sir," they say in unison. "Goodnight, Mom. Goodnight, Dad."

"Goodnight," I shut the door softly.

"They're going to miss you," Sarah whispers. "I'm going to miss you." She frowns and her chin wrinkles as her bottom lip quivers. She's fought back tears all evening and she's done.

"Let's go to bed."

2
FAMILY FUN OR FAMILY FAIL?

SARAH

The next morning, my cell phone alarm startles me awake. I forgot to turn the damn thing off for today. So much for sleeping in.

I drag myself out of bed and shuffle into the en suite bathroom. After using the bathroom and washing my hands, I stare at myself in the mirror as I picture the day ahead.

"Make it count," I mutter to myself. *I guess it's time to start my day.* On the vanity, I grab several bottles of medication. Depression, anxiety, and ADHD give me a full cocktail of daily medication. I'm only 28 years old. I can't imagine what my medicine cabinet will look like when I'm in my 60s. I fill the plastic cup beside the sink with water and swallow down the small handful of pills. As I'm finishing up in the bathroom, Ryan walks in to start his morning routine.

"I'm going to make some coffee. You want some?"

"Yeah, sure. Thanks." I give him a chaste kiss and walk out of the bathroom, through the bedroom, and make my way to the kitchen. I need coffee and I need it now. I find the largest mug we own and stick a dark roast K-Cup in the machine. Sweetener and milk and I'm all set. I brew a cup for Ryan as well and carry both steaming beverages to the dining table.

Ryan joins me at the table, and we doom scroll Tiktok as we sip our coffee. He sends me funny animal videos and all the cute otters while I scroll Booktok and Kinktok. It's funny how closely those two niches can be related.

"Hey, watch this with me," Ryan says, standing up and pulling his chair closer. On his phone, a video titled 'Songs Turning 20 in 2020' is queued to play.

"Oh my god." I roll my eyes. He starts the video, and we jam out to early 2000s hits. Damn, I feel old now. He's downright giddy with some of the songs on this list. And suddenly, my mood falters. "I'm going to miss this," I admit aloud.

"Miss what, babe?"

"This. Just sitting next to you and bullshitting. I like having you around, even if we're not doing anything." He stands and gently pulls me up from my chair and wraps his arms around me.

"It's not forever, babe. And I'll get mid-tour leave to

come home and visit." It's supposed to be reassuring, but I'm apprehensive. I pull back and look at him, my eyebrows pull together in frustration.

"They've just started allowing travel again. What if the Covid numbers spike again and the governments restrict travel again?"

"We can 'What if' all day, but we won't know until the time comes. Let's make the most of the time we have, okay?"

"Okay, okay. I know. Let's get the girls up and get ready to go. We can take them to the trampoline park and the arcade," I suggest as I walk down the hall to the girls' room.

"I need to go to the store. There's some stuff I still need to pack for my trip. Carlos said we can't wear uniforms off the compound and headquarters is at a different location. I'll need civvies while I'm driving back and forth."

I pause at the kids' room door, continuing our conversation, "You know, I remember a time when you gave me shit for using first names with people I worked with when I was on active duty."

"It's different with Officers," he retorts.

"Yeah, yeah. What clothes do you need?"

"A few polo shirts and slacks should be fine."

I open the door to Callie and Rebecca's room and turn on their light. "Time to get up, girls. We're going to breakfast, then it's Family Fun Day."

"Family Fun Day?!" Rebecca sits up. "Where are we

going?"

"Trampoline Park and arcade," I tell her as I walk across the room to her dresser and begin taking out clothes for the day. Once I've picked out an outfit for Becca, I pick something for Callie. Usually, they choose their own clothes, but we have a busy day, and I don't need them taking forever to decide on clothes.

"Dad and I are going to hop in the shower real quick. You two get dressed and finish cleaning up your room. I want to leave in 30 minutes or less. Callie, get up!"

"I'm up," she sits up slowly and rubs her eyes.

"Don't fall back asleep," I warn.

I leave them to get ready to go and walk back to our bedroom to get ready for the day. Ryan already has the shower running to get the water warming up. I strip down and toss my pajamas in the dirty clothes basket. As I walk past Ryan to step into the shower, he smacks me on the ass.

"Hey!"

"What?" He smirks and smacks me again.

"That hurt!"

"No, it didn't. You big baby," he teases. I stick my tongue out at him and turn to step into the shower. He laughs at my antics.

We wash up and he steals all the warm water. Once we're all clean he suddenly turns off the water. *Guess we are done.* He steps out and hands me my towel. We dry off and I walk back into the bedroom to dress for the day. My phone chimes with an alert. I sit down on the bed to check my phone and Ryan takes the opportunity to push me back and climb on top of me.

Propping himself up on one arm, he takes my phone from my hand and sets it on the bedside table. After setting my phone down, he parts the towel covering my freshly showered body, baring me to him.

"We're supposed to be going out," I remind him.

"We'll be quick," he leans in and presses his lips to mine, parting my legs with his knee. I glance towards the door, checking the lock. Of course, it's unlocked. One of these days, the kids are going to catch us. "They're probably not even out of bed yet," he says, kissing the sensitive skin behind my ear. "Relax."

Ryan kisses his way down my body, teasing and caressing my flesh. He massages my breasts and pinches my nipples. Each touch sends a pulse of heat to my core forming an ache only he can relieve. I groan in frustration, and he chuckles at me. Still, he shows mercy, moving further down my body and positioning his face between my thighs. I feel his warm breath on my sex. This is torture. I lift my hips, reaching for his touch, but he grips my hips firmly and pins me down.

"So much for 'quick'," I snark. Ryan smacks me on the side of my ass and raises his eyes to meet mine.

"Talk back, and you don't get to cum."

"Fine," I acquiesce and watch as he lowers his mouth to my throbbing clit.

RYAN

She loves to talk back. If we didn't have plans, I'd draw this out much, much longer.

I flick her clit with my tongue. Short, quick, teasing licks. Her hips push against my hands as she tries to get closer, trying to take what she wants. I alternate long, languid strokes of my tongue with short, quick flicks. There's no pattern and it will drive her crazy. I slip a finger into her pussy and rub her G-spot. She's fighting back moans, trying to stay quiet, but that just won't do. I suck gently on her clit and insert a second finger into her wetness. I plunge my fingers in and out, applying pressure to her G-Spot with each pass. Her legs start to tremble, and I know she's close.

"I'm gonna cum," she whispers. I twist my hand, fingers massaging her inner walls as she clamps down with her orgasm. Juices rush out of her, coating my fingers and soaking the bed. I lick her once more from her slit to her clit, teasing the over-sensitized skin. "Please fuck me." That's all I need. I flip over to her stomach and smack her ass.

I slip inside of her easily, she's soaked from her orgasm. I thrust slowly a few times, enjoying the feeling of her tight pussy. "Rub your clit," I order. "I want to feel you cum on my cock." She reaches a hand beneath her and strokes her clit. I thrust into her faster and harder. Moments later, her walls tighten and she cums on my dick.

SARAH

He makes me cum twice more before we switch positions. He turns us over and I climb on top. I hate being on top. Not that it doesn't feel good, but I don't like the way I look up here. After two kids, weight gain, weight loss, and weight gain again...I'd rather not. But he says he likes what he sees, so here we go.

"I love the way your tits bounce," Ryan says, pulling me back to reality. I get into a rhythm and my confidence grows. His breathing quickens and his thighs tense beneath me. He's close. I keep my rhythm and I feel his body tighten more and more as he inches closer to his release. "Don't stop," he says. "I'm gonna cum." He groans, grabbing onto my hips and holding me in place. After he comes down from his orgasm, he pulls me down, chest to chest, and kisses me softly.

"It's gonna get on you," I tell him, and his eyes track the length of our bodies and stare at where our hips meet.

"I'll get a towel. Ready?" After seven years of marriage, it's fucking strategic to try not to make too much of a mess on the bed. We're better off buying new sheets than trying to wash them because my ADHD-addled brain can't ever remember to switch the laundry.

"Yep, ready." I climb off of him *very* carefully and roll onto my back. I have my legs raised and parted, and to be honest, I look like a turtle stuck upside down. Ryan comes back with a towel and helps clean me up. "We need another shower," I whine.

"Nope. I want my cum leaking out of you." *Well, fuck.*

As Ryan predicted, the girls were not ready to go when we emerged from the bedroom. Becca's initial excitement for the day appears to have vanished as she snores softly. *These kids...*

"Wake up!" Ryan shouts, and Callie sits up immediately. Becca, however, stays in bed. "Rebecca, you don't get to have fun if you don't get up."

"I'm up, I'm up." She rubs her eyes and rolls over, scooting toward the edge of the bed. Finally, both kids shuffle from their room to use the bathroom and get ready to go.

Twenty minutes later and we are finally ready to leave. Becca's excitement has returned and asks every five minutes if we're there yet.

"Not yet. Just a few more minutes," I repeat for the umpteenth time.

"You're so annoying," Callie whines, crossing her arms over her chest.

"No, I'm not! You are!" I roll my eyes and resist the urge to threaten to go home if they don't behave.

I don't like it when they behave this way, but today is important. Pick your battles, right?

"Look, we're here." Ryan backs into a parking space and shifts into 'Park'. "Let's have a great day."

And we do have a great day. The kids laugh and play and show us tricks. Rebecca has become quite the little daredevil as she somersaults on the trampolines. Callie tells us to watch as she jumps higher and higher.

Two hours at the trampoline park and we take a break for lunch. A lot of places are still at reduced capacity for COVID-19 protocols, so I put us on the online waitlist for Red Robin. The restaurant has pretty good appetizers, and with little kids, you really can't go wrong with a burger and fries.

Callie tries to Monopolize Ryan's time with tic-tac-toe while I help Becca with the maze on her paper menu. The food arrives a short time later and the girls devour their lunch. Ryan and I finish our food and pay the bill, and we're off to the next stop on our Family Fun Day.

RYAN

"How many cards?" the cashier asks.

"Three, please," I look over to Sarah and smile. Arcades are so much fun, and I always get her a card of her own to play games. She earns tickets while the kids play the other games. Each trip to the arcade is like a personal challenge for her: how many tickets can I get this time?

"That'll be $58.42." I pull my wallet from my back pocket and pay for the game cards. The cashier hands me the cards and I distribute them to my girls.

"Once it's out, you're all done," I tell them, and they're off. Callie plays racing games while Rebecca rides the little rides. Sarah loves coin-drop games and this digital fishing game. She lights up like a kid on Christmas when she plays.

An hour later, the cards are dead. The sucker I am, I reload an extra thirty minutes of playtime on each card. Anything to see my girls smile. Sarah is already up to over five thousand tickets. Rebecca and Callie have around a thousand each. Rebecca hit the jackpot on a game for five hundred tickets earlier. It was so awesome.

As it gets closer to dinner time, the arcade gets a bit more crowded. Parents are getting off work and coming in for the evening birthday party set-up. It's time to head out. I rally the kids to pick prizes. This is always a daunting task. Seven thousand and some odd tickets divided by two…It takes what feels like a lifetime, but we finally finish up at the arcade and head home for the night.

"Put your prizes away, let the dogs out, and feed them," I instruct as we walk through the door at home. The kids stumble to their bedroom, attempting not to drop armfuls of arcade prizes on the floor. Then they run down the hall to let the dogs out, leaving the backdoor wide open.

"Close the door," Sarah yells. "It's July in Oklahoma. It's hot and there are a million and a half bugs." The girls apologize and go about their chores.

After eating a big lunch, it's 'Fend for Yourself' night for dinner, which pretty much means cereal. Rebecca eats quickly, hoping to hide away in her room and watch cartoons. Unfortunately, we need to have a family discussion.

"You ready?"

"As ready as I'm going to get," Sarah mutters. "Let's sit on the couch."

"Girls, come sit down in the living room. There's something your mom and I need to talk to you about." We all take our seats in the living room.

"What's up, Dad?" Callie asks.

"Well, remember Mom and I said a few months ago about how I would be going on a trip for a while?"

"Like Mr. Dave?" Rebecca asks.

"Kind of. Remember he went away for a long time, but he came back?" They both nod.

"Daddy has to go away for work," Sarah says. "They scheduled his flight and his trip coming up much faster than we thought."

"When are you leaving?" Callie asks, hurt and anger crossing her little face.

"I need to be at the airport tomorrow morning."

Callie's face turns red and her chin wrinkles, bottom lip quivering. I hold my arms open to my oldest daughter and she quickly crosses the living room to hug me tightly.

"So, we're going on an airplane?" Becca asks.

"No, Sweetie. Daddy is going on an airplane, and he will be gone for a while," Sarah tells her.

"Oh," she deflates. "I want to go on an airplane." I don't think Rebecca's three-year-old brain fully comprehends what's happening. Callie does understand, and she's heartbroken.

I halfway release my embrace from Callie and open my free arm to Rebecca. She walks the short distance across the living room, and I pull her in for a hug as well. Sarah's eyes fill with tears as she watches the exchange, and my heart squeezes in my chest.

It's almost bedtime and our happy day has been tainted by the news of my imminent departure. Sarah and I agree the girls can sleep in bed with us tonight. As much as I'd enjoy alone time with my wife, I think all my girls need to cuddle and spend extra time with me, even if we're asleep.

3
NEVER GOODBYE, ONLY LATERS

SARAH

Ryan's flight is early. The plane takes off at 0700, so his check-in time is 0600 at the tiny regional airport. Fortunately, we live just a few miles away and there are few cars on the road at this hour. Even in a military town, traffic isn't too bad, especially on this side of town.

Two large duffel bags and his laptop bag. That's the extent of his property for the next twelve months. I lock the pups in their crate while Ryan loads his bags into my SUV. Once everything is ready to go, we wake the girls and buckle them into their seats. They're half asleep while we drive to the airport, but reality sets in when Ryan climbs out and retrieves a baggage cart. He opens each of the kids' car doors to give hugs and kisses while I stand to the side and watch. *I can't cry. I must be strong for the girls.* After he says 'Laters' to the girls, it's my turn.

"It's not forever, Babe," he attempts to reassure me. I know it's not forever, but he hasn't even left yet, and it feels like a lifetime already.

"I'm going to miss you," my voice cracks, and I press my cheek to his chest.

"I'm going to miss you, too. But we can video chat all the time. I'll call you on my layovers and as soon as I get to my room." I nod, my face still buried in his chest.

Taking a deep breath, I step back and look at my husband. It's only a year, and he'll be home for leave in about six months. "I think...I think we'll be okay."

"I know you'll be okay." He kisses me gently, but I can't kiss him back. I'm fighting tears and my mouth won't cooperate to reciprocate. Damnit! I won't see him for months. Let me kiss him back! I will my face to relax long enough to return his kiss. He breaks our kiss and presses his forehead to mine. "It's not forever, Babe. Never 'goodbye', only 'laters'."

With that, Ryan gives me another hug and a chaste kiss as our final 'laters'. I watch him push the luggage cart inside as I climb into the driver's seat. Callie is sniffling in the back seat, her face red and tears stream down her cheeks as she cries quietly. Becca watches as Ryan walks away. She's still more disappointed in not flying on the plane herself than her father leaving. It's a blessing and a curse that she doesn't understand as much. She's not upset like Callie, but she appears not to care, even though it's not the case.

I buckle my seat belt and drive home. I've already called out for the remainder of the week. The girls and I need time to cope with Ryan leaving. As we make the short drive home, I think of how to make the time move faster. For now, binge-watching Disney movies and cuddling with the kiddos seems best. I don't want to be around other people, just my girls. This fucking sucks.

"What movie do you want to watch?" I ask as I unlock the front door, pushing it open for the kids to head inside.

"Baymax!" Becca declares.

"Yeah! Baymax!" Callie agrees.

"Baymax it is. Put the dogs out while I set up the movie, please." I love Big Hero 6. S.T.E.M. in movies for kids is awesome to me, and the inflatable robotic nurse is badass, too. I open the Disney+ app on the television and search for the movie. Once it's queued up, I go to the kitchen to make some microwave popcorn.

"Popcorn!" Rebecca and Callie cheer.

"Yes, but you need to have paper towels. No wiping fingers on your clothes," I give them pointed stares to emphasize my point.

"Got it," Callie nods, and Becca grabs the entire roll of paper towels. Not what I meant, but okay.

I microwave two bags of popcorn and empty the bags into one large bowl. I snuggle between my girls on the couch, the popcorn bowl on my lap. The dogs inch closer and closer in hopes of falling snacks. Callie starts the movie, and the three of us find comfort in each other and the silly antics of Baymax and Hiro.

After Big Hero 6 ends, I order grocery delivery. We have been so busy this week that I haven't made it to the store. Fortunately, it is early enough in the day to secure an early evening delivery time. I'm not in the mood to cook, surprise, so I order plenty of cereal, lunchables, and frozen dinners. I also buy some strawberries, cubed watermelon, and carrot sticks. Just because I don't want to cook, doesn't mean we're going to eat like total shit.

The day drags on and on. Around two o'clock, Ryan messages me saying he has arrived at his layover airport. It is a two-hour layover, and he has another four hours or so to fly before he reaches his final destination. He can't call because the airport wifi isn't stable enough for a call and it's so loud I can't hear him anyway. It's so frustrating. We message back and forth during his layover, and it is soon time for him to board his next flight.

Ryan: on the plane. I'll call you when I get there.
Me: have a safe flight. I love you.
Ryan: and I love you A&F.

I let the girls play on their tablets for a while. Ryan and I downloaded some learning games when Callie was sent home from Pre-K during the COVID-19 lockdown. She starts kindergarten in the fall and I want her to be prepared for school. I found a few apps for Becca, too.

Groceries are delivered just after five o'clock. After putting the food away, we have a simple dinner of cereal and fresh fruit. We watch another movie and the kids take a bath before we pile into my bed. Rebecca falls asleep quickly, but Callie lies awake crying softly.

"I miss him, too," I whisper as I cuddle her closer. "But it's only for a little while. He will call us all the time and send us messages."

"It's not fair."

"I know, sweetheart. I wish he didn't have to go. But that's part of Daddy's job. When the Army says he has to go, he has to go."

"I don't like it."

"I don't either. But that's part of why I'm not in the military anymore. We decided it would be better for our family if one of us could always be home," I tell her.

"I want Daddy to be home with us. "

"He only has a few years left in the Army."

"You said it was only a year!" Callie starts to cry.

"This assignment is only a year," I clarify. "He can retire in about six years." I run my fingers through my daughter's hair in an attempt to calm her. After a few moments, her crying has turned to sniffles as her hurt fades away and she drifts to sleep.

A short while later, my phone lights up and vibrates on the bedside table. I shift away from Callie to check the caller ID.

"Hey," I answer.

"Hey, Babe. I didn't know if you'd still be up," Ryan says.

"I couldn't really sleep. And Callie was very upset. She misses you a lot already. We all do."

"And I miss you."

"How was your flight?"

"It was okay. Tim is picking me up, I'm just waiting for my bags. I wanted to check-in. I don't know how long it takes to get to the compound."

"Oh," I deflate. "I thought we could talk longer."

"I'll let you know when I'm at my place. And you need to rest." He makes a valid point. It's been a long day and it was emotionally draining.

"You're right. I'll call you when we wake up."

"Sounds good, Babe. Get some sleep."

"I love you."

"And I love you. Night night."

"Night night."

4
ONLY 364-ISH DAYS LEFT, RIGHT?

RYAN

It was a long day of flying but I'm finally here. Bahrain will be my home for the next twelve months. It's not all bad. Since I'm on permanent party orders, not deployment orders, I have better living arrangements than I would on a normal rotation. Not that I'll be there much. From my understanding, there is a lot of travel within the area of responsibility for my new position.

After collecting my gear from the baggage carousel, I head outside to meet up with Tim. I'm his replacement for this assignment. Fortunately, I was able to arrive in time to shadow him for a few weeks before he heads back to the States. I've never worked with Tim directly, but I've heard good things from other officers in our field. We're a small community in our branch of the Army, if I don't know someone personally, I know someone who does know that person.

Tim pulls up in an SUV and hops out to help me load my bags. "How was your flight?"

"I'll be glad to stop moving for a while," I reply.

"We've got about twenty minutes to the compound. I already have your room information so we can head straight there." He closes the trunk and gets in the car.

"Sweet." I climb into the passenger seat as he buckles his seat belt, and we're off. After a short drive of small talk and a security check at the gate, we pull up in front of one of the residential buildings on the compound. Tim turns off the ignition and we both exit the SUV, grabbing my gear before we head inside.

The facility is similar to an apartment building with exterior staircases and breezeways. Tim leads me up to the top floor to my quarters. We step inside and drop my bags in the living room area. It's a fully furnished one-bedroom, one-bathroom apartment. This is going to be so rough.

"Man, this is awesome," I say as I explore the apartment.

"Yeah, it's great. The Major has two bedrooms in his apartment. The Colonel has a whole townhouse."

"Damn." Tim gives me a rundown of how stuff works on the compound. Mail goes to the post office, not the apartments directly. Drinking water is delivered and I'll have my own vehicle to get around. This is going to be fucking awesome.

"Well, I'll leave you to it. I'll pick you up tomorrow at 0700 so we can get you in-processed."

"Sounds good, man. Thanks a lot." I walk him to the door, locking it as he leaves. It's still pretty early in the day and I want to get over jet lag as quickly as possible, so I find ways to keep myself busy until bedtime, starting by putting my belongings away. I connect my devices to the building wifi and send a message to Sarah informing her I've arrived at the apartment and I'm getting set up. It's a nine-hour time difference so she's still asleep for now.

Around four o'clock, I head out to find something to eat. There's a market a short walk away. I pick up a few essentials and grab a to-go sandwich and salad for dinner. In my apartment, I pull up Netflix on my computer as I eat dinner. While I'm throwing my trash away, a call comes in on my messenger app.

SARAH

I wake up and check my phone for a status update from Ryan.

Ryan: I'm at the apartment. Call me when you wake up.

No need to tell me twice. I open my messenger app

and hit the button to video chat. After what feels like an eternity, the call connects, and I see my husband's handsome face through the little screen.

"Morning, Babe."

"Morning. I'm glad I can talk to you again. Yesterday was one of the longest days of my life." We chat about his afternoon and he gives me a video tour of his apartment. He's living the good life over there. The next twelve months are going to be so hard for him…not.

"Daddy!" Callie shouts, grabbing for my phone. Look who's awake.

"Hey, Boo Boo," Ryan says.

"When are you coming home?"

"Well, I just got here. I have a year over here." I let Callie talk to Ryan while I let the dogs outside and take my medicine. I could go for a cup of coffee, too. A few minutes later, the bickering starts.

"I want to talk to Dad!" Rebecca yells. Guess who else is awake.

"I had the phone first!"

"I'm going to take it if you don't stop arguing," I declare, walking through the bedroom into the bathroom to take my medicine. The arguing stops, for now. "What do you want for breakfast?"

"Pancakes!" Becca votes.

"Yeah, pancakes," Callie agrees.

"Pancakes it is." And off I go to the kitchen to make breakfast for day one of Ryan's absence. Only 364-ish to go.

5
IT'S LIKE GROUNDHOG DAY, UNTIL IT'S NOT

SARAH

Time passes slowly and every day seems to be much like the day before. Wake up, get ready for work, get the kids ready for summer camp, work, pick up kids…over and over again. Our evenings involve quick dinners of kid-friendly meals so I don't have to hear the kids argue and complain about meal choices. We spend a lot of time sitting on the living room couches. The girls watch television while I binge-read smutty romance on my phone or doom scroll Tiktok. We call Ryan before bed, disrupting his sleep. It's an eight-hour time difference and it's difficult to find time to talk.

Life carries on this way through the summer. When school starts back in August, the first two weeks are virtual learning. This COVID-19 world is a pain. I work a full day and have to homeschool Callie after work. We order in or stop through a drive-thru many nights during these early days of the school year. I frequently lock myself in my room and cry from the stress of single parenting, homeschooling, and working full time.

"I can't do this," I sob as I vent to my mom on the phone.

"Yes, you can." Her words are kind but firm. Mom didn't raise a quitter. "Ryan has already been gone for six weeks. You're that much closer to him coming home."

"But it's taking forever. Time is moving so slowly."

"Stay busy and try to have fun with the kids. It'll make time move faster," she advises. As a former military spouse, Mom understands the struggle.

"Thanks for the support, Mom. I'm just having a hard time."

"I know. If things get too hard, I'll come out there. I'm still teleworking."

"I think I'll be okay," I sniffle, the last of my sobs gone as I calm down. We disconnect our call and I go check on the girls. Rebecca is playing dress-up while Callie watches cartoons. My kids are so strong with their dad gone, I need to be stronger for them.

Things start looking better as Callie, Rebecca, and I get into a proper routine. They're still picky about my cooking, so I buy pre-made deli meals from the grocery store, fresh fruit, and other assorted healthy snacks. Becca has been on a string cheese kick. She'll eat five cheese sticks in one sitting, but won't eat anything I cook.

More time passes. It's difficult to get time to myself. The kids and work, that's what fills my day. I don't want to pay for a babysitter but I need time for myself to decompress.

"Go get your nails done," Ryan suggests as I express my frustration.

"When? I work all day and then pick up the kids. I don't want to pay for a babysitter AND the cost to get my nails done."

"Call my parents," he recommends. "I know they'd like time with the girls."

"Yeah, and have them use it against me? No thanks," I retort, rolling my eyes.

"Take off a little early and go after work."

"I'm trying to save my PTO. I'm already working through lunch for therapy twice per month."

"Well, I'm giving you solutions and you're just giving me excuses," he snaps. "It's late and you need to sleep. I'll call you in the morning."

"Okay. I love you."

"Love you." The call disconnects and I set my phone down on the bedside table. I roll over and go to sleep.

The next day, I wake up with a message from Ryan.

Ryan: last-minute meeting. I'll call you when it's over.

I get myself and the girls ready for the day. As I'm buckling Rebecca into her car seat, my phone rings. Once the kids are secured in their seats, I climb into the driver's seat and return Ryan's call.

"Hey, Babe," He answers.

"Hey. Sorry, I missed your call. How was work?"

"It was okay. I have some news." My stomach sinks from the tone in his voice. This isn't going to be good news.

"I don't like the sound of that. Wait until I drop off the girls to tell me." He respects my request, shifting the conversation. I pass the phone to the kids and they take turns playing with the filters on video chat. Rebecca has figured out how to take screenshots, so I always find tons of images from her calls with Ryan. After our short drive and a quick stop for an identification check at the gate, I pull up in front of the school to drop off Callie.

"Say 'laters' to Dad," I say, stepping out of the car and walking around to help her unbuckle.

"Laters, Dad," she says and hands the phone to Becca.

"Have a good day," Ryan says.

I give her a hug and press a kiss on the top of her head. "Have a good day, Sweetie." I watch her walk inside as I climb back in the car and buckle my seat belt. Shifting the car in drive, we're off to the daycare to drop off Rebecca.

Rebecca's daycare is just a few minutes away. I park in front of the building and climb out, open her door, and unbuckle her car seat. Day in and day out, the same routine. It's like the movie Groundhog Day. What will it take to break me out of this cycle?

"Tell Daddy 'Laters'".

"Laters!" She says, blowing a huge kiss at the phone screen. Ryan chuckles and tells her to have a good day as well. I take Rebecca's hand and walk her to the door. I'm not allowed to walk her back to her classroom anymore. Ever since COVID-19 lockdown, there have been a lot more restrictions. I sign her in, give her a big hug, kiss her head, and walk back to my car.

"So, what's the news?" I ask as I buckle, again, and put the car in gear.

"I'm getting extended six months."

"What?! Why?" Angry tears streak down my face.

"My position wasn't advertised for the next move cycle. They extended me until the following move cycle. My position can't be vacant."

"Why is that our problem?" I argue.

"Because the General specifically asked for me to stay rather than short notice task someone else."

I pull into the parking lot of my office building and

put my car in park. Finally, I can look at my husband for this conversation. No, not my husband. A phone screen. A fucking phone screen! He's been gone for two months and all I have is a damn camera phone. I suppose I shouldn't complain. Our relationship started out with Skype in 2013. It was great technology of the time. Now, not so much.

The more I think, the angrier I get. I was prepared for twelve months. I wasn't thrilled. I mean, I married him because I kinda like being around him. But we were both on active duty when we met, and his intention has always been to retire from service. I knew what I was getting into with our relationship. But extended because someone else fucked up?!

"It's fine," I say, trying to convince myself more than him. "We've been apart longer than this before. We're resilient, right?"

"Of course, Babe. You're strong. You've got this."

"I've got this...But you're telling the girls!" I demand. "I won't be the bad guy and break their little hearts!"

"Okay, I'll tell the girls."

I glance at the clock on my dashboard and curse. I'm going to be late. "Shit. I gotta go."

"Have a good day, Babe. I love you."

"And I love you," I say, tears welling in my eyes again. I disconnect the call before he notices. I check the visor mirror and wipe the tears from my eyes and cheeks. That's as good as it's gonna get. I turn off the ignition, grab my purse from the passenger seat, and drop my phone inside. I climb out, lock up, and dash inside. My supervisor isn't in yet so I'm safe. Whew. Let's turn this day around.

6
FINALLY, SOMETHING TO LOOK FORWARD TO

RYAN

"There's a tattoo convention in town next weekend," Sarah says, attempting to sound casual but there's a hint of excitement in her voice. It's been a few weeks since I broke the news of my extension overseas, so I'm glad she's found something to look forward to.

"Yeah? What are you looking to get?"

"I want to finish my sleeve."

"And how much is that going to cost me?" I feign inconvenience. Sarah works hard, too.

"Hey! I make my own fucking money!" And there it is.

"I know. I'm just messing with you. Did you find an artist?" She tells me all about some guy coming to town from Houston and sends me the link to his Instagram profile. "He's really good," I admit. "Did you get a price?"

"Yeah..." she replies guiltily. "$2000." She winces as she looks at the phone screen.

"Otay."

"I can do it?"

"Of course, Babe. We have the money, and you've wanted to finish it for years. Get it done."

"Yay!" She smiles wide. I love her smile so much. Her screen goes dark as she minimizes the video chat. "I'm going to message him now. I want to book my spot." Sarah informs me of a $500 deposit to hold the booking, and she's sending it over CashApp.

"I gotta get to bed, Babe," I tell her, glancing at my clock. It's an eight-hour time difference. It's Saturday, but I work Sundays, and it's getting late here.

"Okay..." Her smile fades. "Let me grab the girls." After a quick 'Night night' to my daughters, I switch off the light and tell my wife 'Goodnight'. Sarah mutes her phone as I set mine on the nightstand. She likes the comfort of hearing me there even though I'm not there.

SARAH

The following week, I drop Callie and Becca off at our friend Dave's house so he can babysit while I'm at the tattoo convention. He's known Ryan since they both joined the Army in 2009, and they have somehow been stationed together ever since.

"Thanks, again, for watching them."

"No problem. I can't wait to see your tattoo when it's finished."

"I know! I started it over two years ago in Texas. I hoped to get back there for that artist to finish it. That obviously didn't happen," I recall as he walks me to the door. "It's supposed to take ALL day. But I'll be back as soon as I can." He reassures me it's no problem. I get in my car and drive across town to the convention center. After I park, I call my bank and request an increase to my daily withdrawal limit on my bank account. Once that's squared away, I head inside.

I find the booth and introduce myself to Tony and his wife, Reina. Tony is already setting up, printing stencils on transfer paper and organizing his supplies for my piece. I make a quick trip to the bathroom before we get started. After about fifteen minutes, we're ready.

After eleven hours of work and a couple of short breaks to grab some food, water, and use the bathroom, we call it a night. Three-quarters of my arm have been tattooed tonight, including my elbow (and holy fuck did that hurt!) I've arranged to come back tomorrow to touch up a few things, but my body just can't handle it anymore and I'm sure Tony's eyes and hands could use a break from all the work he's put in.

I call Dave from my car and let him know I'm on my way. It's just after midnight and I'm exhausted.

Fortunately, he lives just a few miles from us and I can rest. When I arrive, the girls are passed out on his couch, and they've clearly been out for a while. He helps me carry them to the car and buckle them in. I drive home and wake the kids gently. They shuffle inside and crash on the bottom bunk, neither braving the climb to the top. I close the door, let the dogs out for a brief moment, and put myself to bed. I'm zapped.

Sunday's session goes much faster, only about two hours. I scroll my phone while he finishes the work, distracting myself from the sting of my already traumatized skin.

As I'm scrolling Instagram, I come across a local photographer who specializes in boudoir photography. Not just boudoir, plus size boudoir. She empowers women to feel confident in their bodies, regardless of size. Tony finishes my tattoo and applies a protective wrap, and I'm good to go finally! Once I'm back in my car, I immediately send a message to the photographer to schedule a session. Ryan's birthday is coming up and I want to surprise him. By the time I arrive at home, I have a response. She's available in three weeks. That's perfect! My tattoo should be finished healing by then, or at least enough to not look gross in pictures. Ryan is going to love this!

7
CAN WE BE KINKY?

RYAN

Sarah calls me dark and early Monday morning. It is Sunday evening for her, and she's had a busy day. I woke up to at least a dozen pictures of her finished tattoo. She's so excited about it. I also had a message about a 'birthday surprise' and that I 'have to wait to see what it is'. As if we can keep secrets from each other.

"You're really not going to tell me?"

"Nope!" She says, proudly. Sarah sure is fighting her impulses this time.

"I'll believe it when I see it." She sticks her tongue out at me, crosses her arms, and pretends to pout. She's so adorable when she's fake angry. And her nostrils flaring is hilarious. She hates it when I bring it up.

I finally drag my lazy ass out of bed and start my morning routine while she settles in for the evening. She only wakes me up early so I can say 'Night night' to the kids and share the details of her day with me. It's insignificant to some people, but it's important to her. Sarah needs reassurance she's loved and that we're good. If small talk on the phone fills that void, I can do that for my wife. It's weird, she manages small talk with me but hates it with other people. She has a hard time making friends, and it's making this separation a bit more difficult.

In our previous separations, she had friends, clubs, and school, but now it's just her and the kids. I've encouraged her to get out of the house, and she does, but it usually ends up with one or both children upset from leaving the activity. Which, of course, frustrates Sarah and makes her less than pleasant to talk to. She's in therapy and on medication, but it's just too stressful doing it alone. I feel powerless not being there to help her.

After getting lost in my thoughts and subconsciously moving through my morning routine, it's time for work. I grab my wallet, keys, and cellphones, and head down to my car. I'm in for a fun-filled day of meeting after meeting. Yay me...

SARAH

The next few weeks are filled with anticipation. I

scroll social media for ideas to implement in my boudoir session. On Tiktok, I come across several photographers who demonstrate how to take pictures at home. I think I'm too awkward to figure it out and decide I'm definitely sticking with the professional. In my searches, I stumble across some kinkier images. Spreader bars, handcuffs, ball gags, masks, and much, much more. Some of it is a bit extreme for me, but I'm intrigued by other images. After a while, my For You Page has more kink content. Doms and subs making 'thirst traps', enticing viewers to comment, like, and share their videos. I follow a few creators. Their content appears frequently on my feed. Some are sexy and some are educational. Before I know it, I fall down the Kinktok rabbit hole.

"Have you heard of 'Kinktok'?" I casually ask Ryan while we video chat on a Saturday morning.

"I don't know. I watch a lot of different stuff."

"Well, you know how sometimes you spank me while we have sex? And we have those bed straps we've used a few times?"

"Yeah...?" He gives me a 'where are you going with this?' expression. Is this a bad idea? What if he says no?

"Well, some people, couples or whatever the relationship dynamic, have different types of play. Like...more toys and stuff. And some have 24/7 dynamics. The Dom has more control over the sub. But they agree to it. It's not like that book where he made all the rules and there wasn't really negotiation."

"I've heard of all that, Sarah. I just didn't think it's something you're interested in. You make sure to point out your independence." He makes a valid argument. I don't like the idea of being financially reliant on someone else. If it's negotiated in other families and it works for them, great. I don't judge them. Do what works for you. But I have my own issues I need that independence.

"I know. I think part of it is the separation. I'm getting tired of making all the decisions and running things here," I admit.

"I know, Babe. I wish I could make it better."

"Will you think about it? We can learn more and figure it out together."

"I'll think about it," he agrees. He tells me 'Laters' and disconnects the phone. He has dinner plans with a few guys from work. I'm pretty jealous. Not necessarily of him going out. I mean, that's part of it, but he sends pictures of his meals sometimes and the food looks AMAZING. So unfair!

RYAN

I try to process the information Sarah has thrown at me. We've had some kinky sex, but just beginner stuff really. Some spanking and bondage with the under-mattress straps. I've used a few toys on her (toys are tools, not competition), but we haven't ever discussed anything outside of the bedroom.

While at dinner with my work buddies, I laugh and have a good time, but my mind isn't all there at the moment. Part of me is still thinking about my brief discussion with Sarah. Is this something she really wants, or is it fantasy?

After dinner, I decide I need to explore further on my own, Google BDSM. There are sample contracts for Dominants and submissives, Masters and slaves. She would never go for a Master/slave dynamic. I read further and a central message is that a Dominant, regardless of dynamic type, is meant to protect the submissive. Listen to the sub's needs, read body language, really pay attention. If a Dominant feels as though a scene has gone too far, the Dominant has as much right to call a safeword as a submissive. This is something I haven't seen much in the pop culture parts of my research. Many safeword references show the submissives holding all the power to end a scene.

I continue my research and understand more importance of why Dominants should be in tune with their submissives. Sometimes submissives will act in ways to please their Dominants that may push their limits, especially in new dynamics. Sub frenzy is how it is referred to. Submissives are so consumed with excitement and desire to explore new kinks and/or new relationships they often do not maintain their boundaries. This can be scary for even experienced Dominants but can also leave submissives open to exploitation.

My research has given me a lot to think about. I hope Sarah has researched as well, and not just on Tiktok…

8
FEELING SEXY AND...

SARAH

Finally, the day has arrived! My in-laws are babysitting while I go to my much-anticipated boudoir session! I wake up early and have a light breakfast, I don't want to look bloated in these pictures. I wake up the girls and pack an overnight bag for them as they get ready for the day. An entire day to myself! And an evening as well!

After meeting my in-laws at the trampoline park in town to drop off the kids, I drive to the photographer, Ariana's, home. She has converted one of her spare bedrooms into a studio. I park out front and grab my purse, locking my car as I walk up the few steps to her front door. She opens the door wide and greets me warmly, leading me through to an empty area near the dining room so her friend can help with hair and makeup (I'm the worst girl ever.) After layers of mascara and what seems like an entire can of hairspray, I'm ready to pick out some sexy lingerie from the client closet.

Ariana has a closet filled with outfits of all sizes and colors to complement any body type. Ryan loves purple on me, so I make sure to pick out a set he will love. I love black, it's my inner emo kid fighting to get out, so I choose a sexy black body suit thing. I change into my first outfit and we get started.

I'm nervous at first. I'm quite a bit bigger than I was in previous photo sessions, and I'm still not fully comfortable on display. I want to feel sexy, and I want Ryan to find me sexy, that's the point of all this, right? Eventually, I loosen up and find my groove. The poses come much more naturally, and I feel more confident. Soon, the session is over, and I change back into my regular clothes, depositing the used lingerie in a basket to be sent out for cleaning. I thank Ariana for her time and call Ryan from the car on my way home.

"Wow, you look great," he says, taking in my done-up appearance.

"Thanks. It feels weird though. There are like a million layers of foundation on my face. Helped to keep me from looking like a ghost in those pictures." Of course, I told him about the pictures. I can't keep secrets for shit. Ryan laughs at my remark. I'm pale, no doubt about it. Kids were assholes growing up and called me 'Casper', and asked if I glowed in the dark. Fucking pricks.

"Well, you look beautiful with or without makeup." I smile at the sentiment. We chat as I drive home. When I arrive back at the house, we chat a little longer before calling it for the evening. It's bedtime for Ryan since he works on Sundays. We tell each other 'Night night' and disconnect the call.

I doom scroll social media for a while. This has become a routine of mine. When I'm tired of social media, I open my Kindle app and resume the book I was reading. I've been very interested in BDSM romances lately.

I researched before mentioning things to Ryan. I've read blogs from people in the kink community. Couples navigating kink together for the first time, exploring kink as a new submissive...I even took the test to see what kinks I'm interested in at bdsmtest.org. From what I've read, results may change over time throughout a person's kink journey.

While the test says I'm submissive, I'm still unsure. Ryan isn't wrong when he says I focus on my independence. I don't want to rely on another person. I don't want to feel trapped and stay in a relationship because I need someone. I want to be in a relationship because I love the person, and that person is my partner, not superior to me. That's what I have with Ryan. Can we have that in our marriage while also having a Dominant/submissive relationship?

Scrolling Tiktok with Dom and sub thirst traps and reading my smutty novels has filled my mind with new ideas. What types of impact play can we try? I don't think I could handle caning, not anytime soon anyway. Paddles, crops, and floggers sound intriguing. Whips might be too advanced for quite a while. I'm apprehensive about rope play. Bondage in general, all of the yes, but rope...even with safety shears nearby, I don't think I'm mentally ready for that. Probably need to learn more about it. Suspension is a hell-fucking-no from me, thanks.

I read more and more. 'Good girl', 'Daddy's girl', 'Little whore', and 'Pretty Little slut'. The combination of praise and derogatory names for the female characters sparks something inside me. Could Ryan say these things to me? Could I handle it? I want to. Oh, how I want to.

With the kids out of the house and my mind filled with erotic fantasies, I decide to take matters into my own hands, literally. I rummage through the bottom drawer of my dresser and retrieve my wand vibrator. I turn on the bathroom light and crack the door before turning off the overhead bedroom light. I toss the vibrator on the bed and remove my clothing; goosebumps rise across my skin. Climbing on top of the king-sized bed, I find a comfortable position and begin to explore my body.

I caress my hips, my waist, my breasts. I massage my breasts firmly, and my nipples between my thumbs and forefingers. With one hand, I lightly skim my nails down my body, across my soft stomach, and between my legs, teasing the sensitive flesh of my inner thighs. My other hand moves up my neck, wrapping gently just beneath my chin. No pressure, just touch. I long for more. For strong hands to tease the threat of danger but know I'm completely safe.

My hand leaves my neck as my other hand continues to tease the ache between my thighs. So close, but never quite touching. Reaching beside me, I grasp the handle of the wand and turn it on, the hum of the vibrator fills the silent room. I touch the wand to my body. My back arches slightly as the toy passes across my sensitive nipples. Easing the wand closer and closer to my throbbing clit, between my legs, I moan quietly. So close, yet so far away. I move my empty hand up my body and squeeze one breast, and finally touch the vibrator against the ache.

"Yes," I moan into the darkness. "Please," I beg, calling out to the empty room. I pinch my nipple and the slight pain sends me over. I cum, and my juices coat the head of the vibrator as I rub over my pussy, relieving sensation from my over-sensitized clit.

Once my orgasm has passed and I'm ready to get my lazy ass out of bed, I clean my toy per manufacturer instructions, using a sex-toy-specific cleaner. I'm not trying to get any infections, especially down there, if I can prevent it. Ouch and gross...

I get in the shower, taking my time and enjoying the

hot water. When the girls are home, I'm always rushed in the shower, or I wait until they go to bed. They're always arguing, getting into stuff, or won't leave me alone. I can't even use the bathroom without someone knocking on the door or yelling 'Mom! _____ did _____!' I love my kids, but fuck.

After watching some Game of Thrones reruns, I'm thinking it's a good time to call it a night. Checking my phone, I see it's about time for Ryan to wake up, so I text him to call when he wakes up. In the meantime, I start getting ready for bed. Just as I'm pulling back the covers and climbing into bed, my phone rings.

"Hi," I greet him with a sleepy smile.

"Hey,"

"How did you sleep?"

"It was okay. Might take a nap later," he says as he sits up in his bed, a big stretch loosening his tired muscles.

"I wish I could take naps." I roll my eyes and pout. I really am kind of jealous about that. I'm home with the kids and he gets to go out to dinner with coworkers, nap when he's tired, and watch what he wants to watch without worrying about kid appropriateness or interruptions.

"Then take a nap," he says, plainly.

"Have you met your kids? They can't go five minutes without getting into shit," I retort.

"Oh, so when they act up, they're 'my' kids, but when they're sweet and want to cuddle they're 'your' kids?" He teases.

"Make fun all you want. I'm going away for a few months when you get back and see how you like it!" I threaten. Some men would balk at the threat, unsure of how to handle their own children. Not Ryan. He cared for Callie as her parent, not a damn babysitter, when I was hospitalized for depression a few years back. I would never leave my family not because I don't trust Ryan, but because I'd miss them all too much...regardless of how frustrated I get sometimes.

"I just need a break, ya know?"

"I know. When do you get them back tomorrow?"

"We're meeting for lunch. I will be treating your parents since they babysat."

"Awesome. Thank you, Babe. I know you and my mom don't always get along." I smile at the sentiment. That small bit of praise makes me want to do more to make him happy...even deal with his mother.

9
AND THEN THERE WAS CHANGE

SARAH

At Ryan's suggestion, my in-laws have started babysitting once per month. He also hired a housekeeper for me on a bi-weekly basis. It's weird for me to be home while the housekeeper is in the house, so I usually have the worker come out while the kids and I are out for an activity. It was a little easier for the housekeeper when I worked in the office. Ryan has also developed 'Add to Cart' syndrome. As soon as I mention a 'problem' if it's something he can solve with an Amazon purchase, Add to Cart. Two-day Prime Shipping. Flies are bad this summer? Fly swatters, salt guns, and light trap-zapper-thing. Cramps on my period? Electronic abdominal heating pad, vibrate-y thing, snacks, and says to order pizza (and the brownie!) The man is fantastic. And he's all mine!

"Did you eat lunch today?" Ryan asks as he shaves, getting ready for his day.

"I had a microwave meal at my desk. Work has been really busy," I look away from my phone as he turns to stare at me through his screen.

"Working from home is supposed to make things easier, not harder," he reminds me. I quit my previous job because...reasons. Working from home gives me flexibility with the kids and as a military spouse. Win-win.

"I know, I know. But we have deadlines. Everyone else is already working long hours. I need to do my part."

"I'm making it a rule. You need to eat at least two real meals per day. And take a break. Just five minutes an hour, I don't care. Get up from the chair and give your eyes and brain a break."

"Yes, Sir," I mutter to myself.

"What was that?"

"Nothing. I'll take a break and eat like I'm supposed to."

RYAN

That wife of mine is so full of crap. She doesn't take care of herself properly. The kids and work, yeah. She gives it all and leaves nothing for herself. Unfortunately, she complains to me, and she seems unhappy. I need to do something about it.

She said she wanted to try a Dom/sub dynamic. Maybe this is a good chance to do so. I Google a limit list and send her an email, attaching the document.

Fill this out and send it back. You have three days. Take your time and be honest.

I fill out a copy as well, saving it to my documents on my computer. I also draft a set of rules for her to follow in case she agrees to this arrangement. I'd like to have the rules to discuss and negotiate when we discuss limits. While many of the limits are in-person, there are some things she can do without me.

Rules:
1. **Sub will always refer to Sir as "Sir," or any appropriate masculine pronoun, or any established pet name. Words referencing Sir shall always be capitalized.**
2. **Sub will always answer Sir with phrases such as "Yes, Sir," "No, Sir," or "Thank you, Sir." Sub may substitute "Sir" for an acceptable pet name.**

3. **Sub will always retain respect for Sir; however, she will take care to keep the Dominant/submissive nature of the relationship discreetly as required.**

4. Sub shall wear whatever pleases Sir and will change upon request.

5. Sub will at all reasonable times, unless Sir specifies otherwise, maintain physical contact.

6. Sub will not masturbate, cum, or have any form of sexual release whatsoever without express permission from Sir.

7. Sub will always make her body available for Sir's use—moving to give Sir easier or better access as desired.

8. Sub shall not deny kisses to Sir.

9. Sub will always maintain fingernails and toenails. Appointments for manicures will be completed every other week. Appointments for pedicures will be completed at a minimum monthly.

10. Sub will work out a minimum of three times a week for one hour.

11. Sub will drink 4-8 glasses (8 oz) of water daily.

12. Sub will always be open with Sir, taking care

to never sulk or ignore any issues or conflicts.

I think it's a good start. We'll see how Sarah takes it.

As I'm finishing up work for the day, I see a message from Sarah. She has just started her day.

**Sarah: I got your email
Me: yeah?
Sarah: yeah...thanks.
Me: good thanks or bad thanks.
Sarah: good, I think.**

Glad she's not upset. We seem to be on the same page. I would hope so since she brought it up in the first place. I finish up at work and call Sarah from my car, my phone connected to Bluetooth.

"Morning, Babe."

"Morning. So, what changed your mind?" Straight to the point.

"Kinky stuff has been fun in the past. I'd like to see where it goes." And I'd like you to start taking better care of yourself.

"Thank you. How was work?" I tell her about my day as she moves about the house, getting the kids ready for the day. Thanksgiving break is coming up so lots of crafts are coming home from school and daycare, planning care for the kids, or time off from work for Sarah. She's been very conservative about her time off from work. She's convinced if she takes too much time that the kids will get sick or hurt, and she won't have enough time to spend with them without taking unpaid time. She has a habit of catastrophizing things.

Sarah gets the kids dropped off to school and daycare and talks to me about how her new job is going, gossip from her old job, and life in general. Neither one of us particularly cares to talk on the phone, but in a long-distance relationship, what else are we supposed to do? We end our call as she signs in on her work computer. Before I figure out my evening plans, I decide to send her a message to reinforce the Dom/sub idea.

Me: I came up with a list of rules.
Sarah: oh really?
Me: yes. I want you to look it over and give me feedback.
Sarah: will do!

I copy and paste the rules into the conversation. The message shows 'read' immediately, and the little dots bounce as she writes a response. Bounce. Stop. Bounce. Stop. Bounce. Stop.

Me: Shouldn't you be working?

Bounce. Stop. Bounce.

Sarah: I'm multitasking. But I can respond later. On my break.

The snarky tone I can practically hear through that text. I laugh as I type my response.

Me: good girl

I set my phone on the nightstand and change clothes. I need to go to the store and buy some groceries.

SARAH

Ryan: good girl

Those two words just hit differently, don't they? I smile to myself as I put my phone away and focus back on my work tasks. Spreadsheets. So many Spreadsheets.

I do as he says and take breaks periodically, sipping on water and grabbing a snack. At lunchtime, I take time to review his list of rules.

Rules:

1. Sub will always refer to Sir as "Sir," or any appropriate masculine pronoun, or any established pet name. Words referencing Sir shall always be capitalized.
2. Sub will always answer Sir with phrases such as "Yes, Sir," "No, Sir," or "Thank you, Sir." Sub may substitute "Sir" for an acceptable pet name.

3. Sub will always retain respect for Sir; however, she will take care to keep the Dominant/submissive nature of the relationship discreetly as required.

4. Sub shall wear whatever pleases Sir and will change upon request.

5. Sub will at all reasonable times, unless Sir specifies otherwise, maintain physical contact.

6. Sub will not masturbate, cum, or have any form of sexual release whatsoever without express permission from Sir.

7. Sub will always make her body available for Sir's use—moving to give Sir easier or better access as desired.

8. **Sub shall not deny kisses to Sir.**

9. **Sub will always maintain fingernails and toenails. Appointments for manicures will be completed every other week. Appointments for pedicures will be completed at a minimum monthly.**

10. **Sub will work out a minimum of three times a week for one hour.**

11. **Sub will drink 4-8 glasses (8 oz) of water daily.**

12. **Sub will always be open with Sir, taking care to never sulk or ignore any issues or conflicts.**

I don't think using appropriate honorifics will be an issue. Open communication also shouldn't be an issue, or at least I hope not. In a marriage, respect is important. Communication is important as well. I think these are reasonable rules to follow.

Getting my nails done as a rule is interesting. I'm kind of glad he added it. I try to go to the salon regularly, but sometimes life gets in the way. Since I'm single parenting right now, I can't always get time away from the kids to go. I refuse to pay for a babysitter, doubling the cost of the outing.

Water…I guess that's manageable. The working out rule. Fuck my life. Even when I was in shape I hated working out. It's never been an enjoyable activity and I have no fucking clue why people do it. And what is this 'no playtime' shit? Does that apply to him as well? Him with his Only Fans subscriptions. Doesn't he know there's free porn out there? *Fuck.*

Some of these rules really only apply while he's home. I guess that's something we will work on together when he gets home? I take a moment to process what I want to say before I type up my list of concerns, rebuttals, and what I would also like to see. I send the message and put my phone away, logging back onto my computer to finish my workday.

Ryan responds to my message before he goes to bed, but we don't discuss it on video chat during the day. I think it's something we both need to think about and process, not feel pressured to answer immediately.

Ryan: If it helps you reach your water goal, you can use the sugar-free flavor packets.

For exercising, you've expressed multiple times that you're not confident in your body. I want to support you. Start slow so you don't burn yourself out. It won't happen overnight.

Playtime. Do you want this to apply to me as well? We can discuss further.

If you can't follow these rules, there will be consequences:

1 Butt plug for an agreed-upon amount of time with pictures for proof

2 Write lines per infraction.

3 No orgasms

4 Spank yourself and send me a picture of your pink ass as proof

We can discuss more options later.

I read his response after work, and he is already asleep. His response is fair. The consequences are reasonable. Although, how would he know about playtime or orgasms unless I tell him? I message back confirming I accept his terms. I guess we're doing this.

I'm a horrible submissive. This is something I've come to realize after just a few days. The honorific part, no problem. Getting my nails done, no problem. That's the little bit of 'me' time I get nowadays. I'm so inconsistent about him picking my clothes, not that I really go anywhere to wear anything other than yoga pants. I don't work out. I hate it. I tried getting an exercise game for my Nintendo, that lasted about two days. I downloaded a few apps and followed creators on Youtube. Nothing. I can't find the motivation. Since most of the other rules are only applicable when he's physically present, there's not much I can do to redeem myself. I suck at this.

At least he doesn't know about playtime. On nights like tonight, when the kids don't sleep in my room, I find time for myself. I never take long, just a few minutes. I lock my door and hide in the walk-in closet on the opposite side of the bathroom, blocking the sounds from my vibrator.

Press myself down on my elbows, ass in the air, as I reach my toy between my legs. I press the vibrator against my clit and rock against the wand. I let my thoughts take me away as my body climbs, chasing release.

'There's my dirty girl. Are you going to cum on my cock?' I nod and whimper quietly, responding to the thoughts in my head. 'Are you Daddy's little whore?' My legs tremble as my orgasm takes me. Who knew 'Daddy's little whore' would be the password for me to cum on command? Knowing I can't linger too long, I wash up and clean my toy, stowing it away safely in the drawer before I tuck myself into bed. Would he be upset if he found out? Would he enforce his rules?

Days pass and suddenly it's Thanksgiving. Ryan's parents have invited the girls and me over, and I'm just glad not to spend the holiday alone. Halloween was difficult, but not really emotional. Thanksgiving is a time for friends and family, and really hits home that he's away.

The girls and I arrive at Ryan's parents' house around noon. I prepared my sweet potato casserole at home, and just need to pop it in the oven to reheat. The meal is finished around three o'clock and the adults carry the heavier dishes to the table. Becca and Callie set the table, fill drinks, and bring the rolls. We all take our seats and go around the table saying what we're thankful for.

After a pleasant meal, the kids and I head home. I have work in the morning. Ryan's parents offered to babysit but I need to be with the girls. We put on a Disney movie when we get home, Beauty and the Beast this time. What girl doesn't want to be stolen away to a castle with an endless supply of books and yummy food?

I check in with Ryan before bed. Callie and Becca tell him about their day and all the yummy pumpkin pie they ate at Grandma and Grandpa's house. We didn't talk much today while I was with his parents. He tells me how his day was. He didn't have much of a Thanksgiving. It's not celebrated in Bahrain. The embassy was busy with their celebration, so he skipped out and went for sushi instead. The girls are disappointed on his behalf and say they'll make it up to him.

"You can have all the pie!" Callie declares.

"And extra whipped cream," Rebecca adds.

"Thank you, girls. That sounds great." He smiles and tells them to go to bed, instructing me to do the same.

"Yes, Sir," I sass.

"Damn right," he asserts. I sigh, pretending to be annoyed, but inside my heart is full. I think I like this side of him, even just goofing off.

10
IT'S ALL FALLING APART

SARAH

Thanksgiving came and went. The D/s stuff has been hit or miss. I'm pretty shitty at keeping up with rules, and Ryan doesn't really enforce them. I'm starting to wonder if this is something we're cut out for. Am I the problem? Or is it a mutual thing since neither of us is truly committed?

I'm in a discord server with some people from Kinktok and I'm trying to learn more. Sometimes I don't really think I'm submissive. I don't really think I'm a Brat. I don't break rules to push his buttons or to get in trouble for 'funishments', or even regular punishments when I crave attention. I don't follow rules mostly because I forget. I don't like asking for permission to play because I'm embarrassed. As far as the kink community goes, I really don't know where I fit in. The imposter syndrome is real, and I've considered leaving the Discord server so many times because of it.

I'm learning more about Littles. When I read about Littles online, there was some conflicting information for me. A lot of pacifiers, bottles, little-little-age cartoons, and other activities for Littles identifying with younger ages. I even read about some Littles who wear diapers. I don't relate to those aspects of the lifestyle, so I didn't think I was a Little. As I've learned more from other Kinksters and discovered more resources, I've learned about Middles.

Middles are like Littles but relate more to teenagers. They're usually more independent but still crave attention and affection from their Caregivers like Littles do. Middles may be interested in makeup, jamming to awesome music, rebellious behavior (not necessarily Bratting), video games, films, and TV shows targeted for teenage audiences (Cinderella Story and What a Girl Wants! Hell to the yes!) The more I learn, the more I realize that maybe this is where I belong in the kink world. Maybe I don't fit in any of the 'regular' BDSM submissive boxes. I'm not a Brat or a service sub. I'm not a pet or a slave. Maybe I'm a Little, or rather, a Middle. Maybe I don't need the rigidity of other Dom roles. Maybe I need a Daddy!

I continue to research Middles and explore on my own, but I'm still not ready to talk to Ryan about it.

I'm not sure I could take a rejection. He's my husband and we love each other, but rejection sucks in any scenario. It's not time yet.

Christmas is here, and I'm in total hell. No one ever tells you when you're single parenting to buy shit for your own stocking! I bought Santa stuff for the kids. I bought Santa stuff for each of us that's traditional for my side of the family. But other stocking stuffers? Nope! How do you explain to two little girls that Mom and Dad buy a few things and 'Santa' brings the rest? That's what we've told them in the past. So, now they will think Santa forgot about Mommy. I quietly search the pantry for granola bars, leftover Halloween candy, chips, ANYTHING to put in my stocking. I find a handful of items and decide it will have to be good enough. I say, 'fuck it' and put myself to bed, face splotchy and tears streaking my cheeks from the silent tears I've been crying for the past thirty minutes. I sleep like shit. My head hurts from crying so much and I'm not looking forward to the Christmas festivities. It wouldn't be the same without Ryan.

"Mom! Santa came!" Becca climbs on top of me.
"Oof."
"C'mon, Mom!" Callie calls from the living room.
"I'll be there in a minute. Go potty and let the dogs out. Don't need anyone having accidents on the floor

while we open presents. I need to pee, too." I gently push Rebecca off of me and hobble out of bed. I flick on the light switch as I enter the bathroom, and immediately shield my eyes. I use the toilet and wash my hands, take my morning meds, and mentally prepare myself for the day. Walking back into the bedroom, I grab my phone and video call Ryan as I shuffle into the living room.

"Morning," I yawn. "Tell your dad 'Merry Christmas'," I instruct the girls.

"Merry Christmas, Dad!" Both girls shout as they reach for their gifts under the tree.

"Merry Christmas."

"Wait," I scold. "Stockings first. Then I will pass out gifts. Let me grab a trash bag." I can't stand trash all over the floor. Even just a few pieces of wrapping paper stress me out for some reason. I think I picked it up from my dad. That man got mad about everything when I was a kid.

The girls dig through their stockings while I retrieve a trash bag from the kitchen. They laugh at some of the items and squeal in delight at others. I repeat 'no' over and over as they ask to eat candy.

We open presents, which take a grand total of fifteen minutes. Make the obligatory phone calls to thank family members for gifts and wish everyone well for the day and into the coming new year.

I spend late morning and early afternoon cooking. Christmas 'dinner' is ready around three o'clock. I plate up food for the kids, and we sit down at the dining table. Becca won't eat dinner. I worked so hard to make alternatives to traditional holiday dishes because of her picky habits and it still wasn't good enough. I cry. For the second time in less than twenty-four hours, I cry. I call Ryan at some ungodly hour for him and lose it. The weight of the past six months crashes down.

RYAN

She's lost it. She's officially lost it. I don't mind her waking me up at two in the morning to cry. She's overwhelmed, feels unappreciated, and life generally sucks right now. I wish I could take some of her pain. But all this does is make me feel like shit that I can't be there. I listen to her cry. I tell her it'll be over soon, that I'll be home to visit in a few months. I ask to talk to the girls and tell them to be good for their mom; That Sarah is doing her best and it's been really hard. Callie feels guilty and Rebecca just wants to make her mom smile. They're good kids. Once I've calmed everyone down, I try to go back to sleep. I finally drift off, but it's restless.

Sarah calls me as she goes to bed. We don't talk, we just fall asleep together on the phone. A few hours later, I wake up and start my day. I reflect on everything she said last night. I know things are hard right now. I've tried to make things easier for her, but I'm not sure what else to do. I wish I could come home and take on some of the responsibility. Every time she get upset, it brings me down, too. It's like life is kicking us both while we're already down. We are resilient, but will this tour break us?

11
AND TIME GOES ON AND ON (AND ON)

SARAH

Months come and go in a slow-motion blur. Most days, I forget what day of the week it is. My days with the girls have become so routine. Working from home, I live in my pajamas. I order pizza far more than I care to admit, but I keep healthy snacks in the fridge, so we won't die of scurvy or anything. If I'm completely honest, I'm probably depressed. I was diagnosed several years ago, and I take my meds every day, but life has ways of getting you down. I had a military career, but we decided the kids needed stability. And I have a thriving career now, so that's a win, right? I've put on weight since Ryan and I got married, but I have a healthier relationship with food and my body gave me two beautiful children. My life is good, but my partner is gone. My love is gone. What's the point in this if he can't be here with me? God, I'm thinking like he's dead. *I just want my husband home.*

"Mommy! Can we watch a movie tonight?" Becca's excited voice pulls me from my spiraling thoughts.

"Yeah, Sweetie. What do you want to watch?"

"Ghostbusters!" I smile as she jumps up and down excitedly.

"No!" Callie argues. "I'm tired of that movie."

"You can pick next if you want. It's Friday, so we can have a movie night," I offer. "And next week is Spring Break, so you'll have lots of fun at camp."

"Yay!" Callie and Rebecca run off to get ready for school and daycare. I make myself a cup of coffee and sit at the table, checking the different notifications on my social media apps. When the girls are ready to go, we get in the car and call Ryan.

"I sent you an email," he says as he answers the call.

"Hello to you, too."

"Hi, Dad!" The girls shout from the backseat.

"What was the email about?"

"Read it later and find out," he says, knowing the anticipation is going to drive me crazy.

"Asshole," I mutter. Becca and Callie take my phone and play with filters as they talk to their dad. The daily routine continues, dropping off Callie and then Rebecca before heading back home to log in to work. Ryan and I talk while I drive. When I arrive back home, I relax on the couch and mute the call while I scroll through the fifteen videos Ryan has shared on Tiktok. I unmute and thank him for the videos. I need the laughs.

"So, what is the email about?" I ask, slightly nervous to read it.

"Read it and find out."

"Can't you just tell me?"

"Fine, but only because we need to talk about it and we won't have time later," he acquiesces. "We've been very inconsistent about anything with a Dom/sub relationship."

"Yeah. You've mentioned before that I'm a shitty submissive," I retort. "I wasn't sure if you're actually interested or if you were saying so because you think it's what I want."

"I just think it's a lot; trying to start a new dynamic in our relationship while we're also navigating a long-distance relationship. Either one of those scenarios would be challenging. Both together, it feels impossible."

"Then why did you agree to try in the first place?" I raise my voice.

"Because I thought we could try."

"So, the whole point of the email was to tell me you don't want to have a D/s dynamic with me?" I'm hurt. It feels almost like I've been broken up with. He's right, we've been very inconsistent, but how does this resolve anything? Maybe if I had spoken up in December about the Middle stuff, it may have been easier. Then again, maybe not. "It's fine."

"We can try again when I get home," he attempts to console me. I'm disappointed and slightly heartbroken, but I'll survive.

"I gotta go. It's almost time to log in to work. Love you."

"And I love you," he smiles softly before ending the video call. I fight the urge to launch my phone at the wall. I'd rather not fork out a thousand dollars for a new phone.

RYAN

Once again, I've upset her. It's damned if you do, damned if you don't. If we continue the half-assed dynamic we've been attempting, neither one of us will feel satisfied we're getting what we need from it. Ending it, or rather pausing it, she's hurt. Sarah has self-esteem issues and she's probably doubting herself in a million different ways right now. The 'what if' voice in her head will nag her over and over, and nothing I say will make it better. We will talk ourselves in circles until we're both pissed off and the situation is worse than we started. Another reason I decided to talk before she signed on for work rather than waiting. Downside: it likely will eat at her all day. I can't do anything right sometimes.

The longer I think about things, the more I wonder why she wanted to change things in our marriage. Is she unhappy? We can play in the bedroom without a dynamic outside of the bedroom. Is she only interested because of Tiktok and the way the lifestyle is portrayed on social media? Regardless, I don't feel like I can fully support a shift in our relationship from halfway across the world. That will have to wait.

SARAH

Throughout the day, I stew in a mix of hurt and fury. It's difficult to focus on work. I tackle some easier tasks, not wanting to make any mistakes in more important areas of the project. I stumble through and log off at the end of my duty day. I often work late, project deadlines and all, but my mind isn't there today and I can't afford to make sloppy mistakes.

Thoughts flood my brain, wave after wave of hurt and resentment. He said he'd try. He agreed. He sent the list of rules! He was fully on board and committed. Or that's what I thought. Why didn't he communicate all this sooner? Why get my hopes up and then give up? We've been shitty about the entire thing anyway, but he's giving up rather than working on improvement?

You know what? Fuck him. If he doesn't want to do this with me, I'll do it on my own. I reach out to my Discord server and vent. I'm met with a lot of support. Offers of virtual consensual hugs, words of encouragement, and comforting emojis. This group has become like a family to me.

User12: you don't need a Dom to be a sub.

Me: sometimes I wonder if I'm really a sub at all.

35_User: well not all Littles are subs either.

Me: yeah, I've been learning about that.

User12: and you can be submissive in the bedroom but not live it 24/7. That's completely valid.

User12: kink is customizable. It's whatever works for you and any partners involved.

AB_User: 100% I'm a Little and I don't really do anything else BDSM. And I don't have a Daddy right now.

Me: thanks everyone. It's nice to know I'm not alone.

And it really is nice to know I'm not alone. Not all Littles, or Middles, need a Daddy (or Caregiver). Some Littles need or want more from a Caregiver than other Littles. I often feel like a fraud because I don't age regress, but my friends from the kink community reassure me that's common and quite normal as well. Not all Littles age regress. Not all Littles need or want Caregivers. Littlespace/Middlespace looks different for everyone even though there are often similarities. The more I talk to others and learn about the lifestyle, the more I learn about myself. The more I learn about myself, the easier it is to pull myself out of this pit of depression I keep finding myself in.

RYAN

It's been a few weeks since Sarah and I talked about putting our dynamic on hold. She seems to be doing a bit better. She's been doing her makeup more and goofing off on Tiktok. She bought some new clothes. She seems to be embracing the alternative girl clothing style from her teen years. She even set up an appointment to get her hair done in some bright colors. She's never done that before. Her previous employer had a policy against it. It's nice to see her doing better. I wonder what changed.

12
A (CHOKED) BREATH OF FRESH AIR

RYAN

It's Ramadan in the Middle East which means my mission is slowing down for a few weeks. With the lull in ops tempo, my chain of command has decided it is the best time to take my mid-tour leave. Sarah and the girls are so excited to see me. Sarah and I are taking a trip to Universal Studios for our anniversary this year. Well, early anniversary. Our real anniversary is over the summer, but I'll be back overseas by then. We also have some fun activities planned for the girls. A trip to Great Wolf Lodge in Dallas. It's a few hours away from Oklahoma, but the surprise will surely be worth the drive.

My flight back to the States is booked and my bags are packed. My work buddy is going to drop me off at the airport. Everything is all set. The last item on my checklist is a COVID-19 PCR test within twenty-four hours of my flight. My flight is scheduled for midnight tonight. My COVID-19 test is in an hour and should take about two hours for the results to come back. Just gotta kill time while I wait.

SARAH

I got out of the house on time to drop Callie off at school and Becca off at daycare! Actually, we got out early! I'm so proud of myself. And Ryan's flight gets in Wednesday evening around dinner time. It's a great day. With the extra time, we make a quick stop at Starbucks. I order a venti white mocha for myself and a vanilla bean Frappuccino for the girls to share. As I'm pulling out of the parking lot, Ryan calls.

"Hey!" I answer cheerfully, "How are you doing?"

"Hey, Babe. I have some news."

"Well, when you say it like that, it doesn't sound good."

"Yeah. My assignment list came out today." I forgot about that. How did I forget?

"So, why do you make it sound like bad news?"

"There are only three CONUS posts," he says.

"Only three Stateside bases?" I repeat.

"Yep." To make it clear, this wouldn't normally be an issue. And now that I work from home, I have the flexibility to relocate and keep my career. But only three Stateside locations don't give much hope. There's a strong possibility we could move overseas.

"What next? You're going to tell me your COVID-19 test came back positive and you can't come home?" I bite out, sarcastically.

"Actually..."

"No! Fuck, no! Anything else?" Angry tears stream down my face.

"Dad's not coming home?" Callie asks from the backseat. *Fuck*. In my frustration, I didn't even think to hold off this conversation until I could speak to Ryan alone.

"I took another test to make sure that wasn't a false-positive. Those results should be back in an hour."

"So, if the new test is negative, you can come home?" I ask.

"Yes," he confirms.

"Ok. Well, everyone needs to think happy thoughts and have good vibes."

I drive to Callie's school on autopilot, Ryan's news weighing on my thoughts. I pull up to the drop-off line and put my car in park. I unbuckle Callie, give her a hug, and tell her to have a good day. I climb back into the car, buckle myself in, and drive to Rebecca's daycare. I unbuckle her, Ryan tells her he loves her and to have a good day. I walk Becca to the facility entrance and wait outside per COVID-19 procedures, before heading back to my car.

My drive home is spent in frustrated silence. I want to speak with my husband about the information he dropped on me, but I don't want to cause an argument. I can't take a day feeling like I swallowed a rock because we have an unsettled disagreement.

"When will you have an answer about the second test?" I ask, breaking the silence.

"Another hour or so. It's fine, Babe. We can reschedule."

"Yeah, I guess that's why we got trip insurance, right?"

"Exactly." I finally turn into the driveway and remove my phone from the charging dock. I stare at the screen, taking in my husband's handsome features. I just want him home.

"I'm going to put on a show or something to decompress before I log in to work. I need to clear my head."

"Ok," he responds, his clipped tone indicating he's upset about something.

"Let me know what you find out."

"I always do." He disconnects the call, and I get out of the car. *Please let him come home.*

A few hours later, Ryan messages me.

Ryan: the second test was inconclusive.
Me: what the hell does that mean?
Ryan: I took a third test. Those results are due in

an hour.
Me: fuck.
Ryan: I'll let you know.

Inside I'm screaming. Outside, I'm trying to stay calm. I already picked up the girls for the day, and I can't give any indication there's a problem. It's time for dinner, so I head into the kitchen. Tasks will keep my mind occupied, so I'm not focused on his test results. Anticipation causes me so much anxiety sometimes. I make sandwiches for dinner; carrot sticks and apple slices on the side. This has become one of my favorite meals. It's easy, yummy, and pretty healthy. I think that sets a good example for the girls. Well-balanced meals and treats in moderation (we love our cookies and ice cream cones!)

Callie, Rebecca, and I watch TV while we wait. They still don't know there is a possibility Ryan may not make it home this week. It's best to keep us all distracted. Becca and Callie don't need to be disappointed until we have an official answer, and I need to reduce my anxiety. This waiting game sucks.

The girls have decided Octonauts is no longer their favorite show. Now, it's all about Bluey. It's a really cute show and I enjoy it as well. Although, the Octonauts theme song is pretty catchy. The episodes are short, and as we are on our fifth episode my phone rings.

"I'm glad to finally hear from you," I tell him,

getting up from the couch and walking into the bedroom.

"It's been a hell of a day."

"Yeah, no kidding. What did you find out?" I've been frantic as I've waited for the news all day. I dreaded the thought of telling the girls their dad wouldn't be home for at least 3 weeks. Fourteen-day quarantine period, rescheduled flights, etc. Travel policy from the State Department says a person can travel for up to twelve weeks with positive COVID-19 test results, following the two-week quarantine period. So, at least three weeks, and that's if his leadership could still accommodate his leave. They could say he's needed back. 'Needs of the Army' and all that. Ugh.

"We're on the way to the airport now," he says.

"Thank god," I breathe a sigh of relief.

"I'll be in around dinner time tomorrow."

"Yay! We can have pizza and relax."

"Sounds great, Babe. We're pulling up to the airport now. I'll text you between flights."

"Otay. I lovers you!"

"And I love you." We end the call and I rush into the living room.

"Daddy's on his way home!" I announce joyfully.

"Yay!" Both girls shout happily, bouncing in their seats on the couch. Just a little longer.

RYAN

I hate flying. Not the flying part. Being in airports all day, tiny seats on the airplane, hours and hours of no personal space. It is hell. But I will be with my family again. For thirty days, I will be with my family. I will sleep in my bed in my house, not a thin, lumpy mattress in an apartment provided by my employer. I should be grateful. Most soldiers don't have living quarters as nice as mine while serving in the Middle East, but they're also on different orders than I am. It's a bittersweet arrangement.

After hours and hours traveling, twenty hours to be more precise, I finally arrive back in Oklahoma. I grab my bag from the overhead compartment and exit the aircraft. I make a quick stop to use the bathroom and reapply my deodorant. It has been a long day, after all. I head straight to the exit, skipping baggage claim. Since most of my belongings remained at home, I didn't pack much for the trip. As I step outside, I search the arrival/pick-up lane for my Dad. Sarah is at home with the girls. We want to surprise them a little, so Dad is driving me home.

When I finally locate Dad's truck, I walk down the sidewalk to meet him. He sees me as well and climbs out to greet me. He opens the door to the back seat and holds out a hand.

"Let me take that, Son."

"I've got it, Dad," but he reaches for the strap of my duffle anyway. I let my old man take my bag and toss it in the back of the truck. He shuts the door and turns to look at me.

"We missed you, Kiddo," his voice cracks as he pulls me in for a big hug. I hug him back.

"Missed you guys too." He ends the hug, clapping me on the back.

"Ready to go?"

"Ready." Dad walks around to the driver's side as I climb into the passenger side of the truck. He asks me about my flight. "I think I'll upgrade on the flight back. Those are cramped seats for a twelve-hour flight."

"Oh, I bet."

The drive is short from the airport to the house. As soon as I step out of the car and shut the door, I can hear the yaps of the dogs barking at the door. I grab my bag from the backseat and walk up the path to the front door. My hand on the doorknob, I take a deep breath before I turn it and slowly push the door open. How much have things changed between us in nine months?

13
THE SPICE IS STILL SPICY (AND THEN SOME)

SARAH

He's finally home. After nine months, I finally get to see my husband's handsome face, and not through a digital screen. Ryan barely makes it five steps into the house before our daughters spot him.

"Daddy!" Both kids run full sprints at Ryan. Taller than when he left, Callie's forehead smacks him in the stomach as she barrels in for a hug. Becca is at hip level, hugging him from the side. His body sways as he holds both children closely.

"We missed you," Rebecca says.

"Don't ever leave again," Callie demands.

"You know I can't promise that. But I'm almost done over there. And I'm visiting for a whole month!"

The kids bounce up and down excitedly, and Ryan gazes at me from across the room. I walk toward him and lift my face to his, as he bends slightly to press a kiss to my lips. "Hey, Babe."

"Hey." The girls finally let go of their dad, leaving him and me standing in the entry of the living room staring at each other. "I ordered pizza. It should be here any minute now."

"Great. As good as the food is over there, pizza just isn't the same as the Americanized stuff."

"I'm going to head out," Ryan's father calls from the doorway.

"You don't want to stay for pizza?" I ask. He's been so understanding and polite, letting us have our intimate family moment, the least I can do is feed the man.

"I'm good. I'll pick up some food on the way home."

"Thanks, Dad. I really appreciate you being there for me."

"Of course. Just glad you made it home safe." With that, he turns and leaves. It's the four of us again. That's such a great feeling.

Ryan takes a quick shower as we wait for the pizza to be delivered. As he's walking out of the bedroom, the doorbell rings and the dogs start barking.

"It's just the pizza!" I tell the dogs, as if they understand. The girls feed the dogs and set the table as usual. "What do you want to drink?" I ask Ryan.

"I'll just drink water. Thanks, Babe."

We eat dinner and talk. Ryan tells us about his flight and tells the girls some of the plans we have while he's home.

"But I have school," Callie frowns.

"Yes, but we have special permission from school for you to spend time with Daddy since he's been gone so long," I explain, and her frown quickly turns to a smile. We spend a nice evening together. Ryan 'enjoys' a few episodes of Bluey with us. What's his problem? It's a cute show!

"It's time to get ready for bed. Brush, floss, mouthwash. And change into your pajamas."

"Okay…" they say, slowly getting up from the couch and rubbing their tired eyes. Our bare-footed little girls pad down the hall and start getting ready for bed.

"You get ready, too," Ryan tells me.

"I'll help you tuck the kids in."

"I'll take care of it. Go," his commanding tone indicating this is non-negotiable.

"Yes, Sir." I walk into our bedroom and get ready for bed. I take my evening medication, brush my teeth, and use the toilet. I brush my hair and pull a hair tie onto my wrist. Giving myself a once-over in the mirror, I decide it's as good as it's going to get before he comes to bed.

Stepping out of the bathroom into the bedroom, pulling the door closed to just a crack behind me, I see Ryan sitting on the bed. His expression gives nothing away, which is more nerve-wracking than showing his thoughts and emotions.

"You okay?" I ask.

"I'm great, Babe." He stands and walks towards the bedroom door, flicking the switch beside the door, cloaking the room in darkness; the glow seeping through the crack of the bathroom door is the only light, saving me from disorientation. "Clothes off, and lie your back," he orders, nodding towards the bed.

I comply, both anxious and excited. We've played before. He's been dominant in bed before. And even though he said he wants to put our dynamic on pause, I think he still considers play time acceptable. Sounds good to me.

I lie on my back, arms in a neutral position at my sides. I keep my body as neutral and relaxed as possible, giving Ryan access to move and manipulate my body as necessary. He crosses the room and opens the drawer where our toys are kept. The sound of him rummaging through the drawer as he searches for the items he intends to use on me makes goosebumps rise across my skin. I'm filled with anticipation, fighting the urge to sit up and watch what he's doing. He stops his search and pushes the drawer shut. Beside the bed, Ryan drops several items on the bed. I turn to peek at his selection, but he slaps me on the thigh. A warning.

"You'll find out when I want you to."

"Sorry."

"'Sorry' what?" He prompts, leaning in closer.

"Sorry, Daddy." *Oh, shit.*

"Good girl," he whispers in my ear, not hesitating at the honorific. My pussy clenches. Those two words. *Fuck.*

RYAN

She lets out a soft sigh when I say 'Good girl'. I don't think she even realizes she does it, but I love the sounds she makes. I love how wet she gets. I love that she's mine. And right now, my dirty girl wants to be tied up and tormented before she gets a good, hard fuck. We'll discuss this 'Daddy' business later.

I pick up a blindfold off the bed, one of the items I chose for tonight. Leaning over the bed, I slip the blindfold over Sarah's head and position it over her eyes.

"Don't move that," I warn, "or you don't get to cum tonight." She pouts and makes some annoyed sound. I smirk to myself as I continue preparing what I have planned for her. "Arms up above your head." She follows my instructions, stretching her hands towards the headboard. I position the straps on the bed to secure her wrists and also allow maneuverability of her body. I bind her wrists in the cuffs on the straps. I pay attention to placement, allowing space between the cuff and her wrist, preventing injuries to nerves or lack of blood flow. Some areas of the lifestyle are new to us, but safety has always been our priority. We've established safe words, even though we haven't had to use them. Our play is pretty tame, especially from what we've both seen from others. While kink looks different for everyone, basic priorities are safety, consent, and being in the right headspace.

She pulls against the restraints and writhes against the bed. The anticipation is really getting to her now. I walk around to the foot of the bed, remove my clothing, and look at the gorgeous woman in front of me. Her curvy body with large breasts and a soft belly, pale skin covered in brightly covered tattoos, and cascades of thick, vibrant hair frame her beautiful face. My wife is stunning. She can be so nice, almost to a fault. But tonight, I'm going to treat her as the not-so-nice girl I know her to be.

I grab the crop off the bed and lightly skim the leather across her bare flesh. Sarah shivers involuntarily, her body tensing as she fights to stay still. I trace the implement across her stomach and carefully snap it against one breast. Teasing her more and more, I make my way down her body. I brush the leather lightly across her aching clit, barely touching her sensitive skin. I flick the crop to each of her inner thighs, and she hisses at the sting left behind.

I toss it to the floor before leaning in on my elbows, spreading Sarah's thighs, my face inches from her cunt. I grasp her hips firmly as she attempts to bridge that final gap. The space between my lips and her pussy. To ease the ache that's been building and building.

"Please," she whimpers.

"'Please' what?"

SARAH

This man is maddening. I can't move my arms and he has a firm hold on my hips. I can't reach any shred of relief. He wants me to beg and plead. I'm halfway there, saying 'please', with a whimpering tone to my voice. Not begging yet, but I'm closer with every moment he neglects my needy body.

"Please, Sir," I respond, gritting my teeth as I fight the urge to talk back. He'll end this now and I won't get an orgasm at all if I smart off. Damn him.

"Good girl," he praises, closing the short distance between his mouth and my pussy. A teasing flick of his tongue before gently sucking on the sensitive nub. I moan quietly, careful not to let my sounds of pleasure carry throughout the silent house.

He devours me, making up for lost time. I climb closer and closer towards climax as he licks and sucks and nibbles. But it's not enough. He knows it's not enough. He's still teasing me. Building me up without letting me tip over the edge to cum.

"Put a finger inside me," I beg, "please." Releasing his hold on my hips, Ryan slips a hand between my thighs. Continuing his ministrations, he strokes a finger up and down my slit, coating his fingers in my wetness. I'm so close. I just need something inside me.

Fuck!

Finally, Ryan takes mercy on me. He slowly slides one finger inside me, rubbing against the slick flesh of my vagina. He licks my clit with short, firm strokes as he massages my G-spot. A few short moments later, my pleasure tips over the edge.

"I'm gonna cum," I moan, my orgasm overtaking me. I succumb to wave after wave of pleasure as Ryan's tongue works wonders and my pussy clenches against his finger as he steadily pumps in and out of me. But we're not done yet. Sometimes I wonder if Ryan would fall into pleasure Dom territory.

He stops the torment of my over-sensitized bundle of nerves and shifts his position between my legs, and I feel him press up slightly. Inserting another finger into my pussy, he thrusts faster, the heel of his palm hitting my clit with each thrust. Faster and faster, he works his hand, and my legs begin to shake. My climax is sudden, a gush of fluid soaks the bed as I cum, stifling a moan. Ryan has made me squirt before, and I'm not confident in my ability to maintain discretion if I moan audibly during such an intense orgasm. He removes his fingers and spanks my pussy several times. I welcome the slight pain that accompanies smacks on wet flesh.

RYAN

Her pussy is drenched, and there is a huge wet spot on the bed. I love making her squirt. Her cunt is extra sensitive afterward, and she will cum and cum and cum.

"Roll over," I order, grasping her hips and filling her over, mindful of the straps above her. She scrambles to her knees, her body angled down. Her forearms are pressed to the mattress as her stability is limited with her hands bound. I smack her ass and she jolts forward at the unexpected contact. Reaching over across the bed, I pick up a leather paddle. It's padded on one side and solid on the other. Sarah won't know which side to expect, and that should intensify her experience. I rub the paddle across each ass cheek, and she presses backward against me.

"What are your safewords?" I ask.

"Yellow to slow down and red to stop."

"Good girl." With the padded side of the toy toward her bottom, I raise my hand slightly and land a mild smack to one cheek. I repeat on the other side, alternating cheeks and building power and speed behind each other until her skin has warmed up. The increased blood flow and endorphins released should make more intense toys and harder impacts easier to withstand.

Once I'm confident her body is ready, I check in. We don't use the traffic light system for check-ins during play. Just simple 'Are you comfortable to continue?' And she will answer 'Yes' or 'No'. After confirmation Sarah is ready to proceed, I flip over the paddle and spank her ass with a firm swat. She jerks forward at the increased pain, but quickly moves back into position. Smack after smack, switching between padded and solid sides of the leather paddle, and massaging her stinging cheeks, I redden Sarah's ass.

"Yellow," she says.

I immediately halt my actions to check-in. "What happened?"

"I don't want to stop playtime, but I'm done with that toy." I drop the paddle on the bed, remove her blindfold, and gently unfastened the wrist restraints.

Once she's free, she rolls to her back and reaches for me. I shove the toys aside and position myself above my wife, spreading her legs with my knee. I lean down and press my lips to hers, lifting her leg as I slide my hard cock into her slick pussy. I take her soft and slow, building up harder and faster. I make her mine all over again, making it count as our time together is limited. She cums over and over, and when I cum, I hold her close. I never want to let her go.

14

ANNIVERSARY TRIP MIDDLESPACE

SARAH

Ryan has been home for almost two weeks, and it's been amazing. He spends time with the girls while I work during the day, much-needed time. Between this school and that school as part of his military training, field training, temporary overseas duties, and now this assignment, Ryan has missed so much of the girls growing up. Especially Rebecca. He takes the kids to activities. Yesterday they went to the trampoline park. Callie showed off her cool moves and Becca played in the tube area with the slides. They went to Chuck E Cheese a few days ago. I wish I could go hang out. *Damn work*.

I'm finally cooking again. I love to cook, but the kids are picky so there's not much point. Now, I can cook all of Ryan's favorites. I love doing things to make him happy. Maybe the girls will let me cook more when he leaves again. Ha, right.

One of the things I've been looking forward to the most is our anniversary trip. Ryan is taking me to Universal Studios. I've wanted to go since they opened Harry Potter World ten years ago! I get to be a kid again and live the magic of a kid going to Hogwarts. Our flight is tomorrow. He's packing some stuff while I'm working. I'll finish up when I log off, and then we drop off the kids and set out for the hotel. Early flight!

We meet Ryan's parents for dinner. The girls eat five bites each and ask for dessert, typical. In a good mood, I give in. We pay for dinner, treating Ryan's parents since they are babysitting for four days. After dinner, we switch car seats and hand off bags for grandparent weekend. Clothes, a few favorite toys, toiletries, snacks, etc. to get the girls through the weekend. Once everything is loaded, we strap the girls into their seats, give hugs and kisses, and thank Ryan's parents again. Callie is sad and worried we won't come home. We reassure her we would be home in just a few days, and she could call any time to check-in. That makes her feel better. As usual, Becca is jealous that she can't go on the airplane. Silly girl. Once everyone is calm, it's time to go. We watch as Ryan's parents pull out of the restaurant parking lot and climb into his truck.

We drive about an hour to Oklahoma City. It was easier to get a nonstop flight from OKC than to have a three-hour layover flying from the regional airport to OKC. We were also able to get an earlier flight since the regional airport didn't have connecting flights for the 7 a.m. departure we are scheduled for. We grab our overnight bag from the truck and check in at the hotel. It's already 8 p.m. and we need to be at the airport around 5 a.m. to park and get checked in. It'll be an early night tonight. We relax, television playing in the background as we share funny videos on Tiktok. When a kinktok video comes up on my FYP, it reminds me of something.

"Did you know there's a lifestyle club here in OKC?"

"Oh yeah?" Ryan pauses the video on his screen. "How'd you learn about that?"

"I saw some videos about dungeon etiquette and read some articles. There are some people in the Discord I'm. They go fairly regularly. I thought joining a club, even temporarily, might be a good way to meet people and observe. I don't think I'm ready to play in public. If I'll ever be ready."

"Otay, Babe. Send me the info." I blink at him for a moment, surprised I didn't need to convince him further. Focusing, I open the browser on my phone and pull up the website. I copy the link and text it to him before he has a chance to change his mind.

The lifestyle club, aptly named 'The Club', is a BDSM club located here in Oklahoma City. In the

'About' section, it is identified as a members-only club with a hyperlink to 'FAQs' to learn how to join.

On the 'FAQ' page, there is a lot of information. One of the options to gain membership is to be vetted by a current member. Even with this option, to gain membership a person must attend at least three venue-hosted munches and pass a background check.

Another option is through a recruiting event. Recruiting events are held on a recurring basis, usually quarterly. During recruiting events, the venue is open by invitation to potential members who have filled out a form expressing an interest in joining and have completed a background check. The Club focuses heavily on the privacy and safety of all members. Also, for this reason, recruiting events do not have active play. The attendees may tour the venue, similar to an open house. Different areas are available to be explored and various amenities are included in membership. The bar, alcohol-free, is open and patrons are free to meet and greet with staff and any members in attendance, as well as ask any questions prior to joining.

Well, it doesn't look like we will be going any time soon.

Calling it a night, I plug in my phone, take my evening medication, and brush my teeth before changing into my pajamas and snuggling beneath the blanket. Ryan gets ready for bed and climbs in beside me, switching off the light, and pulling me in close.

The alarm rings stupidly early. It should be illegal to wake up before the sun. I slept like shit, waking every hour. It's normal for me. I'm so afraid to miss my flight, my body says 'fuck you'. I'll sleep on the plane. I follow my morning routine like a zombie. Ryan and I share a shower, and we pack up the overnight back. We drop the room key at the front desk and head out to the truck. Passing the Starbucks drive-thru, I pout when I observe they're still closed. But my white chocolate mocha!

We park at the airport and walk a short distance from the garage to the departures check-in to drop off our bags. A short delay at security as the early morning time has fewer security gates open. Once we're cleared, Ryan beelines for Starbucks. My hero. It's smooth sailing from here.

We finally arrive in Florida and check in with the resort shuttle. With COVID-19 restrictions, it's easier to stay at a resort on property than to stay off. Besides, it cuts down on transportation costs. The shuttle ride is short, and when we arrive at the resort I'm in awe. Our hotel is Venice-themed and even has a boat to shuttle us to the parks. It's so beautiful and I'm so excited! We get checked in and change clothes. Travel clothes and amusement park clothes are not the same. Ryan and I queue at the pier for the shuttle boat. I'm almost bouncing in excitement.

RYAN

Sarah has so much joy on her face already. She's wanted this for ten years, and I'm proud to be the man to make her dream a reality. The boat arrives and we board, I pull her close and she intertwines our fingers as we hold hands. The breeze blows her hair around as the boat travels toward the main entrance. She swats the unruly strands with her free hand, and I laugh.

"Stop it." But her protests make me laugh more.

The boat docks and we climb out, walking to the gate. Themed shops and restaurants line the boardwalk, and Sarah points excitedly at several.

"Can we go there?" she asks, pointing to the Wonka-themed restaurant.

"We will see." She pouts at my response, unsatisfied. Her head whips left and right and left again as she takes in the sights around her. After we scan our tickets and are admitted into the park, Sarah grabs a map, and her eyes scan the page.

"There!" She points, "We have to go there! Let's go!" She hastily folds the map and grasps my hand, tugging me down the path. The woman is on a mission. She dodges patrons right and left, damn near running me into them.

"Slow down," I tell her. She stops for a moment and turns to glare at me. "Okay, okay." And we are off again, Sarah weaving us through the crowd. As we move further into the park, I can see rooftops peeking through the crowd. We finally reach the entrance to Diagon Alley. "Oh, wow." Sarah stops walking and gazes out at the scene in front of her. A wide smile on her face, yet her eyes glisten with unshed tears. "You otay?" I reach for her, and she shuffles a few steps towards me. I rub my hand up and down her back a few times.

"I'm great," her chin wrinkles, "I'm just really happy. Happy tears are weird." She laughs, wiping the tears welling in her eyes.

"Yeah," I kiss her softly. "Ready?"

"Ready."

SARAH

I'm here! After ten years of waiting, I'm here! Ryan follows around to each Harry Potter attraction. We wait in line for ungodly amounts of time, but it's worth it. The Hagrid rollercoaster is amazing. Not just for the ride, but also the scenery while patrons are in the queue. The Hogwarts castle. Oh my god! I wish I could be a student. Combating a wave of motion sickness, we agree not to ride the castle ride again, but it was so awesome! Butterbeer is a bit overrated, sorry not sorry. It's too sweet!

The dragon at Gringots is a great touch, adding to the magic. The shops have cool souvenirs, and I can't decide what to get. Ryan buys me a badass Death Eater shirt. It's black and gray and totally fits my style. We ride so many rides and eat so many snacks. My heart, and belly, are full.

This trip has fulfilled so many needs I didn't realize I had. So many needs we both have. We have always tried to make time for each other. Date night at least once per month was a regular thing for us. But we were locked down for COVID-19 for over two months before Ryan left to go overseas. We couldn't go on date nights during that time. It was the four of us all the time. Which was nice, especially with his looming overseas tour. But no kid-free time really takes a toll.

I haven't had much kid-free time at all in over a year. Between lockdown and Ryan being gone, it's all me. The overnights Ryan's parents babysit once per month are my only break. And that time is getting depressing. I don't really have any friends, so I mostly just spend the evening alone. Pretty pathetic, huh?

Aside from kid-free time and alone time with Ryan, this trip is allowing me to embrace my inner child (without those pesky parents to rain on my parade). I can enjoy my vacation and be carefree without my dad getting pissed off, and my parents fighting. I can ride what I want without burdening anyone. I can laugh, play, and have fun without being 'disruptive' or 'misbehaving'. I can be the kid I didn't get to be, and I can live my childhood dreams with the park's addition of the Harry Potter attractions. Is this Middlespace?

15

WATER PARK BEFORE THE WATER WORKS

RYAN

I've been home for about three weeks now, and Sarah's mood is changing each day the closer to me leaving again. We're taking the girls to Great Wolf Lodge in Dallas tomorrow. They're excited. They love the water and constantly want to play in the sprinkler. To prepare for the trip, I've instructed both kids to gather items to pack. Callie has her stuff neatly layered in a stack on the floor while Rebecca just has a pile of stuff tossed together. Nurture vs nature at its finest. Sarah has most of her stuff packed minus toiletries and medications. I'm almost finished with my packing. I also have laundry in the wash and have packed up a few of the items I brought with me from Bahrain. That's definitely contributing to Sarah's souring mood.

The next morning, we wake up bright and early.

Sarah finishes getting the girls ready while I load the truck. We drop the dogs off at the doggie hotel and stop for breakfast. After we eat, we make the three-hour drive to Dallas for our mini family vacation.

We get checked in, wolf ears and all (Sarah wanted her own pair of wolf ears). We drop our gear in the room and explore the resort. A wand shop for the quest games, an arcade, a stuffie workshop, Starbucks, an ice cream shop, a candy shop, a swim store, and so many more things to see and do. And of course, the water park!

SARAH

As we're exploring the resort, we make our way back to the lobby. There is a massive window that looks into the water park. Both kids race towards the window and lean their faces close to the glass. Their breath fogs up the window as they watch the families play.

"Can we go?" Becca turns to Ryan and me, pointing at the bustling area.

"Yeah! Can we go?" Callie asks, her excitement mirroring her little sister's.

"Not in those clothes," I answer.

"Race you upstairs!" Callie challenges.

"Oh no you don't," I chide. "Walk." We walk to the elevator and return to our room. The kids change clothes faster than I've ever seen. Priorities. Ryan and I take turns changing into our swimsuits in the cramped hotel room bathroom. Once everyone has changed, we exit the room and make our way back to the elevators. Both girls watch the numbers count down as the elevator descends to the second floor. The lift stops with a ding, and the doors part. Becca rushes forward, almost colliding with another family entering the elevator.

"Excuse me. I'm so sorry," I skirt past the family, rushing after my daughter. I scurry after Rebecca, Callie dashing to keep up and Ryan carries forward with his usual stride. Becca finally stops, a teenage boy working at the park entrance halts her to confirm height before she's allowed entry.

"She can ride everything except these," the teen says, motioning to a board with pictures of the slides inside. "Let's check your height," he motions Callie to the measuring chart posted on the wall. She stands up tall, falling about two inches short of the requirement for the biggest slides. "Okay, they have the same restrictions." The kid walks to the little kiosk by the door and retrieves two yellow wristbands corresponding to the girls' heights on the chart. He secures the bands and trims the excess. "Have fun," he waves us through the door, and we're off for a fun-filled family adventure.

As we walk through the water park, the din of the crowd, splashing water, and music overhead immediately overwhelms my system. You're fine, I remind myself. It'll be fun. I know it will be, but I'm already overstimulated. I hate crowds and loud noises. I hate water in my ears and dripping on my face. I'm always paranoid about losing track of the kids. I'm so on edge, and we just got here. *Deep breath. Deep fucking breath*. I grab a few towels from a cart as we scan the chaos for a few chairs to stash our stuff. We luck out, scoring some seats in view of the kids climbing structure. The girls will be able to play without us following them around

Kiddie slides, dump buckets, hot tubs, and fruity drinks; wave pool, lazy river, and pizza, we wrap up our day at the water park. Drying off, Ryan and I remind the girls over and over that we will return another day. We don't live too far and we can make the trip again. Reluctantly, both children dry off, pouty frowns on their little faces. We deposit the used towels in the bin as we exit the park. The blast of the air conditioning in the resort area makes me shiver, and I quickly shuffle toward the elevators. So cold.

RYAN

I watch Sarah run toward the elevators, both kids in tow. The bell dings and the doors part, and my three girls rush inside. Goosebumps cover their skin.

"I really wish we could bring the towels upstairs,"

Sarah complains.

"We probably can."

"Yeah, well, I'd rather not get charged a stupid amount of money for cheap ass towels." The elevator slows to a stop and the doors open. Callie and Rebecca run out, sprinting in the direction of our room. Callie taunts Rebecca after beating her in their unofficial little race. I unlock the door and we all step inside.

"Get washed up," I tell the girls. Not needing to be told twice, Becca turns on the water and the steam fills the tiny bathroom. "Don't get water all over the floor."

"Yes, Sir," both kids answer, closing the door. I can hear wet bathing suits drop to the ground and small splashes as they climb in and sit down in the bottom of the tub.

I quickly change out of my trunks, retrieving a pair of pajama pants from our bag, and draping the damp swim shorts on the sink until I can hang them up in the bathroom. I grab my phone and climb up onto the bed, lounging back, and checking my notifications from the afternoon.

"I'm getting out of this suit," Sarah digs through the overnight bag to find her pajamas. She tosses the dry clothes on the bed and fights to get out of the tight, wet fabric. "This is why I hate one-piece suits," she grits her teeth, inching the damp suit over her soft belly and hips. I casually watch from behind my phone, a combination of amusement and growing arousal. Once she's out of the cold, wet garment, I set my phone on the nightstand and reach for her.

"Come here." Sarah eyes me warily. She picks up and dons her shirt as she rounds the bed.

"What's up?" I grasp her hand in mine and pull her toward me. She steps forward, lifting one leg to kneel on the bed, then the other, straddling me. "I'm gonna fall off," she says, nodding to her knee perched at the edge of the bed. Hands on her hips, I push up on my feet, shifting my bottom half over further into the center of the bed. Her knee is no longer in danger of sliding off.

"Better?"

"Much." Hands on her hips, I rub circles into her flesh over the cotton of her shirt. I let go of her hips and run my hands up her sides. The light pressure tickles her and she wriggles in my lap, giggling as she tries to swat my hands away. "Stop it." I keep going. She squirms and tries to get away, fighting the tickling. I hold her in place with one hand and tickle her with the other. She squirms and wriggles right off my lap, flopping sideways onto the bed. I roll her onto her back and climb on top of her. I take both of Sarah's hands in one of mine, restraining her gently. I lean forward, my lips to the curve of her neck. I growl playfully and she continues to giggle, trying to buck me off her. I lift my face and switch to the other side of her neck. Her hips stop bucking against me to push me off and she starts pressing her hips against me. Her giggles and laughs slow, and instead releases a soft moan. As I kiss her neck, she writhes against me. Her playfulness is gone as she's filled with longing.

SARAH

I never understood the growling before. I've seen videos and I've heard audio clips, but I always experienced second-hand embarrassment more than anything else. Ryan's growling…it's not like that. It's not a showy 'I'm dominant and growly, look at me.' No. It's very much in the moment and comes naturally. He responds to me, and my body very much responds to him. My pussy fluttered almost immediately. It's fucking insane. I'm so turned on; I can almost feel my clit throbbing.

I raise my hips to his, trying to grind against him. He pulls away slightly before dropping his pelvis back down. He kisses me passionately and tries to mark my neck. Over and over, we repeat this song and dance until he is rock hard and I'm aching to be filled.

"Can you fuck me now?"

"You want me to fuck you now?" He's mocking me but I'm too horny to care. "Not yet" he kisses me deeply and reaches a hand between my thighs. He slides two fingers through my folds, coating them in my slick arousal. He pushes his fingers inside me, pumping in and out hard and fast, fucking me with his fingers. Ryan's hand brushes against my clit with every thrust of his hand, rubbing my g-spot over and over.

My body climbs higher and higher, and I shatter, covering my mouth to stifle my moan as I soak his hand.

Lingering flutters of my orgasm remain as Ryan shifts his sleep pants down over his hips with his free hand and kicks them off somewhere across the bed. While undressing he continues to coax ripples of pleasure from my body. Transitioning smoothly, he repositions himself between my legs and lines up the head of his cock at my entrance. Gliding the head up and down through my folds, he coats himself in my slick arousal. Up across my dripping flesh, Ryan teases the sensitive nub before sliding the tip down to dip just barely inside my pussy. I wrap my legs around him, pulling his pelvis closer as he strokes up and down again. Positioned at my center, I pull him close, the tip finally sheaths into my warm, wet channel. Fully inside, I tighten my hold, legs squeezing tightly around his. He tilts his pelvis and his cock angles differently inside me. I groan at the sensation, relaxing my legs and releasing my hold on him.

RYAN

She unwraps her legs and I can finally move. I raise her thighs and thrust in and out, watching her tits bounce beneath her shirt. The faster and harder I fuck her, the more they bounce. Fuck, I love her tits. I let go of her left thigh and reach down to play with her breasts. I slap her breasts and pinch her nipples, Sarah's soft moans spurring me on.

I want to make her moan louder, to make her scream, but she holds back. Being in a hotel, and the kids in the next room, she won't let go, not fully.

Pumping into her harder and faster, Sarah slides her right hand between her legs, rubbing her clit. Her left-hand grasps my arm, squeezing harder as she chases her orgasm. "Don't stop. Please don't stop," she says, her voice somewhere between moaning and whimpering. I hold my pace, her grip on my arm tightens, and the movements of her fingers flicking her nub are more erratic. She's close.

"Are you gonna cum for me? Be a good little whore and cum on my dick," I order, voice low yet authoritative.

"I'm gonna cum," she whimpers. Her pussy tightens around me, muscles contracting as she climaxes.

"Good girl." I slowly pull out of her and roll her onto her stomach. I press her legs close together and smack her ass once as I climb over her. I position myself to her core and slide my shaft inside her tight channel. Her pussy clenches as I fill her, and aftershocks of pleasure ripple through her.

"Oh, fuck," she says, and I groan in agreement. I fuck her slowly at first. I feel her tighten around me, her body trembles as another orgasm builds quickly. "Don't stop," she says. I do stop, pulling out until only the head of my cock remains perched at the entrance of her cunt. She groans in frustration, and I slowly slide back in. Her body quakes but she says nothing, thinking I won't stop again if she doesn't tell me she's close. I stop again, pull back, and rest my tip just barely inside her. Sarah smacks the bed with her fist, and I chuckle. She lifts her hips off the bed in an attempt to take my full length inside her. I slam my hips forward, burying myself to the hilt. She groans in satisfaction.

"You can cum this time," I say as I begin to move. Without hesitation, she slides her hand between her thighs and rubs her clit, frantically chasing the orgasm I stole.

"Oh fuck, oh fuck." Her body stiffens, her inner walls clench around me, and her juices coat down my shaft as she cums. "I'm dead," she says, flopping on the bed.

"No, you're not." I wring three more orgasms from her before positioning on her hands and knees, taking her hard, and finding my own release. After I cum, Sarah leans up on her knees and I pull her close, pressing kisses to her shoulder. "Ready?"

"Not really," she says, leaning down on her forearms while I slowly pull out of her. I climb off the bed to grab a hand towel from beside the sink. "I can't hold it," she says, scrunching her face as she clenches her kegel muscles. "Noooo!" Cum drips out of her and onto the bed. I press the towel against her, preventing any more mess. "You're sleeping on the wet spot!"

We get dressed quickly, and just in time. The water shuts off in the bathroom and the door swings open. Our two daughters walk out wrapped in towels, water dripping all over the carpet. We grab clothes for the kids and turn on a movie. We take turns in the shower, the tiny bathroom not exactly ideal for adults sharing showers. After everyone is clean and dressed, we decide to partake in other areas of the resort before calling it a night. Tomorrow, we tell the kids it's time for me to leave again. We're both dreading the conversation and want to stay in this bubble as long as possible.

16
THE TIME HAS COME, THE WIFEY SAID, TO TALK OF DEPRESSING THINGS: OF PLANE RIDES, AND SICK KIDS, OF MURPHY'S LAW AND THINGS

RYAN

Sarah: Callie's sick. Going to the ER

My heart stops as I read the message. My flight just landed in Bahrain. I still have to clear customs and a ride back to the compound. *Fuck!*

Me: my flight just got in. How is she doing?
Sarah: she spiked a fever. Pulse was fast and scared the shit out of me.

Sarah: She's so tired. I can barely keep her awake.

Sarah: I'm so scared

I'm scared, too. I'm fucking useless here. Once again, my family needs me and I'm not there. Sarah is thinking the worst, like she does, and I'm not there to calm her down.

Me: how's Becca?
Sarah: I dropped her off with Dave. Pretty sure I ruined his date night.
Me: he'll get over it.
Sarah: I still feel bad. Of course, this fucking happened as soon as you left.
Me: we're at the gate. I'll message you when I'm back at the apartment. Let me know what the doctors say.
Sarah: yep. I love you.
Me: and I love you, A&F.

I grab my bag from the overhead compartment and exit the plane, shuffling down the sky ramp behind the slow-moving crowd. I clear customs and head outside. Tim drives forward, stopping in front of me at the passenger loading zone. I toss my stuff in the back and slide in, buckling my seat belt as Tim merges into the thru lane. *Off we go...*

SARAH

When military spouses talk about Murphy's Law, it's not a joke. As soon as our service member spouses are unavailable, all hell breaks loose. Unit is in the field? Flat tire. Leadership training out of State? The washing machine dies. Deployed? Kids are sick all the time. It. Never. Fucking. Stops.

When I woke up today and went to get the kids ready for the day, Callie was a mess. Her hair was all stuck to her face and she was all sweaty. I kept the kids home to be on the safe side, but her fever stayed strong. Her pulse felt really fast. *Of course, this happened the day after he fucking left.* So, I called Dave and dropped Becca off at his house.

It's been over two hours since Callie and I arrived at the ER. The triage nurse gave her a fever pack with a combined dose of Tylenol and Motrin. She's so tired and has barely eaten anything. I keep waking her up to drink water. She's nauseous and keeps throwing up what little food she's tried to eat. The Motrin isn't helping, further agitating her already upset stomach. My poor baby.

"Todd, Callie."

"That's us. C'mon, Sweetpea," I grasp Callie's hand gently, pulling her to her feet.

"Hi, Callie, I'm Shawn," a nurse introduces himself, scanning his access badge to lead us back to the patient rooms. "Let's get you back to see a doctor so you can feel better." Callie nods softly, lethargic from her illness. We follow Shawn down the hall, stopping at an alcove with a scale and height chart to check Callie's measurements. He jots down the data and we continue to a small exam room.

Inside the exam room, I help Callie climb up onto the hospital bed. Shawn hooks up the blood pressure cuff and blood oxygen monitor before clicking a protective cover over the digital thermometer. Callie slowly reaches for the thermometer and sticks it underneath her tongue. The blood pressure cuff whirrs as it inflates around her tiny arm before hissing while deflating. The monitor beeps, and measurements are ready for reading. Shawn takes the thermometer back, clicks the release button on the protective cover, and drops it into the trash. He writes the numbers from the monitor on Callie's chart and places the notes aside. He informs us a doctor will be with us 'shortly' and steps out to assist other patients. I message Ryan and bitch about my frustrations, and I message Dave apologizing for interrupting his evening plans. Both men tell me everything will be okay and to focus on Callie.

After thirty more minutes, a doctor finally comes to check on Callie.

"Good evening. I'm Dr. Baxter. What brings you in today?" The mama bear in me wants to bitch this man out. We've been here for hours. I explained what brought us in when I checked Callie in. I explained to the triage nurse. Even Shawn asked! Does no one talk to each other?!

So, I explain, for the umpteenth time. Taking more and more time away from the time my baby girl could be receiving medical treatment. Dr. Baxter listens, taking additional notes on the intake form. The blood pressure cuff, still wrapped around Callie's arm, whirrs in the background periodically. When I'm finished recounting the scary experiences of the day, my heart is racing. My anxiety is rearing its ugly head as I worry over my eldest daughter.

Dr. Baxter conducts a physical exam of Callie. He checks her heart and lungs, ears, nose, and throat, and swabs for COVID-19, flu, and strep. We wait another thirty minutes for the results, and everything is negative.

"Sometimes kids just get sick. It's likely a serious cold. Make sure she rests and stays hydrated. You can alternate Tylenol and Motrin to help with her fever."

We're discharged shortly after Dr. Baxter assigns a bullshit diagnosis of a 'cold', and I walk Callie back to the car. I immediately call Ryan, nostrils flaring with rage as I focus on my breathing, angry tears filling my eyes.

RYAN

"A fucking cold! And he wasn't even sure!" Sarah complains as she cries angrily "We were at the hospital for over three hours and that's it. 'Alternate Tylenol and Motrin. Lots of fluids' blah fucking blah. I could have handled that on my own without waiting hours!"

"How's she feeling?"

"She's tired. I'm going to let her rest more at home. Hopefully, she can sleep it off."

Sarah calms down as she drives. She stops at Dave's house to pick up Rebecca. She lets Callie rest in the car, leaving her phone in the car on video chat so someone is 'with' our sick daughter. The woman is paranoid, but she means well. A few minutes later, Sarah opens the car door and Becca climbs up into her seat. Sarah leans across and fastens her in and kisses her atop her head before shutting the door. She opens her door and slides into her seat, fastens her seat belt, and huffs a sigh.

"I'm so over this day. Becca, wanna talk to Daddy?"

"Yeah!" Sarah unclips her phone from the car dock and passes it back. Rebecca immediately finds the game filters. There's a hamburger game she loves. It's a competition to see who can eat the most hamburgers as they fall from the top of the screen. We finish our second round as Sarah turns into the driveway.

"Carry my phone in, please," Sarah asks, unfastening Becca's seat belt. Becca hops down and scurries to the front door. A few moments later, I hear footsteps as Sarah and Callie reach the door. Sarah unlocks the door and takes her phone back from Rebecca.

"I'll talk to you tomorrow, Babe." It's bedtime for me and there's nothing I can do to help at this point. "I'll call you tonight."

"Ok. I love you," she says somberly.

"And I love you. Everything will be okay."

"I hope so. I'll talk to you later."

SARAH

Callie rests on the couch for a while and Rebecca watches TV in their room. I fill up a water bottle and set it on the floor next to the couch. I grab a bowl as well, placing it beside the water. If her stomach is still bothering her, I'd rather not clean up puke if she doesn't make it to the bathroom.

I sit down and try to relax, but it's no use. I get up periodically to check on Callie, reminding her to sit up and drink something. She finally sits up long enough to eat some toast, but it comes back up just a few minutes later. I give her another dose of Tylenol and she takes another short nap before I wake her up to hydrate.

"My tummy hurts."

"I'm sorry, Sweetie. You need to drink something, or your body won't get better. Do you want some Propel instead?" Since she's been sweating so much with this fever, the electrolytes in the Propel might do her some good. She gives me a weak nod in agreement. I walk to the kitchen and grab a room-temperature bottle from the pantry. I don't like very cold drinks, so non-perishables stay out.

I carry the drink to the living room and twist open the top. Callie has already drifted back to sleep.

"Callie, you've gotta wake up. You need to drink this." I tap her shoulder. "Callie. Callie!" Finally, her eyes open slightly. "Sit up and have a drink."

"What?"

"You gotta sit up, Callie," I speak urgently, trying to remain calm. She's too tired. This is bad. "Can you sit up?" Her eyes open more, and she appears more alert as she sits up, but something is off about her. I hand her the drink and help her, reminding her to take small sips. "Okay?"

"Yeah," she says, a goofy smile crossing her face. It's scary. Why is she even smiling?

"Do you want to try to eat?" She doesn't answer. "Callie?" No answer. "Callie!"

"Huh?"

"Who am I, Sweetie?" I ask, my heart pounding as my panic grows.

She thinks about it for a moment before answering. "I don't know." My heart beats faster, and blood roars in my ears.

"What's your name?" I ask, holding my breath as I wait for her answer.

Again, she thinks for a brief moment. "I don't know," she answers simply. A knot forms in my stomach.

"We need to go back to the hospital, okay? Get your socks and shoes on." I scramble to grab her things and put the dogs away. "Becca!" I call out. "Socks and shoes. We gotta go. Now!" Callie puts her shoes on slowly. I stomp down the hall to check on Rebecca. "Are you ready? Let's go. We need to take Callie back to the doctor." That gets her ass in gear. Two minutes later, we're backing out of the driveway. *Please help my baby.*

After another two hours in the emergency room, Callie is on the mend. Poor thing was fucking delirious from dehydration. Her body was so dehydrated that consuming liquids wasn't enough The doctor, different from earlier, hooked her up to an IV, and every minute she was pumped with saline she felt so much better.

When we get home, I make Callie some toast and she's finally able to keep it down. I'm finally able to relax knowing my little girl is starting to feel better. We call Ryan to say 'Night Night', and I send a message to my supervisor that I need to take a personal day tomorrow. I could log in to work, but I just don't have the energy. Today was too much. I let Callie sleep in my bed tonight, partially for my own peace of mind. I want to know she's safe and still getting better. My catastrophizing thoughts rush to me finding my daughter in a fever coma in the morning. Nope. I'm keeping her close. Maybe we can both rest a little easier tonight.

17

TRY, TRY AGAIN

SARAH

"I wanted to talk to you about something, but I didn't have time before I left," Ryan says. "And then there was all the stuff with Callie getting sick."

"Yeah, it was rough. What did you want to talk about?"

"You called me 'Daddy' during sex. What was that all about?"

"I was hoping you didn't hear that," I cringe. "Just forget it."

"No, I'm not going to forget it. Is that why you've been acting and dressing differently? It's Little stuff?"

"Well…yeah. I wanted to talk to you about it months ago, but you didn't want to do the D/s thing anymore."

"Maybe we jumped in too fast before. Do you want to take it easier this time?" he suggests.

"Otay," I smile.

Later that day, I receive a long message from Ryan.

Ryan: Here is a revised set of rules. I think this will be a bit easier for you to follow.
Rules:
1. **Eat at least 2 *real* meals per day (snacks don't count.)**
2. **Take meds every day**
3. **Take breaks from work throughout the day**
4. **Drink 8 cups of water per day**
5. **Walk 10k steps per day**
6. **No "play time" without permission**
7. **Text me when you go out and when you get home**
8. **Take time for yourself daily (read, write, TV show)**

Well, the meds won't be an issue. I'll try to be better about eating. It's not that I avoid eating. I legitimately forget. I get so wrapped up in work, that I lose track of time. Is that the ADHD time blindness people talk about? Same thing with the breaks. I don't not take breaks on purpose. *How far back can you roll your eyes before they pop out of your head?*

If this man thinks I'm walking 10k steps per day...that's ambitious. I didn't meet that goal when I worked in the office. It's been harder working from home. We will need to negotiate that number, or I'll always be in trouble. Water...I guess that's manageable. He's still slipping the 'not playtime' shit in there. *Total bullshit.*

The texting thing I get. He worries about my safety. And a woman alone, or a woman alone with small children, is a vulnerability. I can respect that. But with what he's said about traffic there, I may request the same from him. Can submissives have rules for Dominants?

Free time for myself? "Hahahahaha!" I literally laugh out loud. I take a moment to process what I want to say before I type up my list of concerns, rebuttals, and what I would also like to see. I send the message and put my phone away, logging back onto my computer to finish my workday.

Ryan responds to my message before he goes to bed, but we don't discuss it on video chat during the day. I think it's something we both need to think about and process, not feel pressured to answer immediately.

Ryan: You need to take better care of yourself. Meals, meds, and water aren't really negotiable. Water you can use a water enhancer squeeze thing or packets, but you need to drink enough. Breaks need to be more frequent as well, but we won't set

a firm number on frequency. I understand you have work calls and can't always step away.

Getting your steps in, let's try for 5k per day and work your way up. 10k is a reasonable goal, though. We'll get there, but we will give it time.

Playtime. Does this one bother you? Let's discuss more.

Free time is important. Maybe not every day. Maybe once a week or twice per month you go get your nails done. That's dedicated time without the kids.

If you can't follow these rules, there will be consequences:

1 Butt plug for an agreed-upon amount of time with pictures for proof

2 Write lines per infraction.

3 No orgasms

4 Spank yourself and send me a picture of your pink ass as proof

We can discuss more options later.

I read his reply after work. The rules are the same as before, so I know what to expect. His response is fair. I guess we're doing this…again.

I'm awful at this. As much as I want to give up control, I'm terrible at following directions and

reaching basic goals. The meals, meds, and water isn't the issue. Walking is constantly a problem. Ryan's punishment for not walking is to write lines. To be 'nice', I 'only' have to write ten lines for every one-hundred steps that I'm short of 5k. Well, I've been averaging closer to 3.5k steps. Fifteen lines per day add up fast!

Ryan isn't a hardass about it, which I suppose I should be thankful for. In fact, I'm so bad about meeting my walking goals, that he's given up on that entirely. I'm not sure if I should be glad or disappointed.

Things are going a little better this time. Ryan has always been amazing about sending stuff if we need it for the house, but now he sends Middle-y stuff. He bought me a fucking Tamagotchi! I squealed in delight when I saw it. He also sent me a Stitch stuffie. It's soooo cute and talks. Note: Do *not* sleep in bed with stuffies that talk. Scared the ever-loving shit out of me!

He fully supports me calling him 'Daddy', even though it felt kinda silly to both of us at first. Overall, I think we're getting there…maybe? I just need to be better at following rules, damnit.

18

IMPOSTER

SARAH

The summer passes with minimal stress. If packing up and selling a house and moving into an apartment alone counts as minimal. Considering the biggest hiccup was waiting for the Power of Attorney to sign on Ryan's behalf, I think things turned out pretty well.

The girls and I are living in a tiny two-bedroom apartment until Ryan gets his new orders. We're on the first floor, so we don't have to go up and down over and over to walk the dogs. But the dogs are infuriating; playing the in-out game wanting to go see everything and everyone outside. But it's only for a few months. Ryan will be home before Thanksgiving!

With the end of our long-distance relationship in sight, my mood has been improving a bit. I've been going out with the girls more and embracing my Middle. We've been to Chuck E Cheese so many times recently, I have random Chuck E swag tucked into nooks and crannies of my car, under furniture, and everywhere in the kids' room. But we've had so much fun, it's worth it.

Me: omg look! *selfie with cat ears*

I post a selfie in the Kink Discord. I bought these at the mall the other day and I finally decided to wear them. I think I look a-fucking-dorable.

User_XYZ: omg those are so cute!!!
Me: right?! I've been feeling Middle-y lately and these were an impulse buy.
39User00: yeah? What does that look like for you?
Me: what do you mean? Like, my Middle?
39User00: yep.
Me: idk. I just kinda find comfort in all the stuff I liked in middle school and high school.
Me: I'll listen to my favorite music from back then. Watch my favorite shows and movies.
Me: I watched the Hannah Montana movie this week. And I've been jamming to Disney radio on Pandora
User12: I totally do the same thing!
39User00: is that Middle stuff though? Or nostalgia?
Me: idk.

Me:. I gotta go. It's dinner time. Adulting calls.

Is 39User00 right? Am I nostalgic and not really a Middle? I mean, this is my personality. Disney and anime, video games, music from my adolescence…it's like I never grew up from that. But after a long day and needing to decompress, or even a great day and wanting to hype myself up, that's what I cling to. But…is that wrong? Is that not being a Middle? Is that just…me?

I feel like an imposter, now more than ever. I felt like a shitty sub months ago when Ryan called me out on it. I thought about leaving the Discord server back then because I felt like I didn't belong. I felt like a fraud infiltrating the community. But my friends in the group said otherwise. I felt seen. I felt validated. And now…someone else has taken that away. Someone who wasn't there last time.

Am I being unreasonable? *Maybe.* Am I overthinking? *Probably.* Am I hurt? *Definitely.* Needing an outside opinion, I reach out to my friend, Tia. I met her on Tiktok during Corona-pocalypse. We still haven't met in person, but I trust her a lot. I found her on Kinktok, so she gets all the spicy gossip.

Me: remember that Discord I told you about?
Tia: All the kinktok people, right?
Me: yeah that one.
Me: I had someone question whether or not I'm

a Middle. The person asked if I'm a Middle or just 'nostalgic' *eye roll emoji*

Tia: that's not for someone else to decide

Tia: kink looks different for everyone. Just because one person's Little side looks one way, doesn't mean all of ours looks the same.

Tia: I totally think you're a Middle!

Me: I'm really thinking about leaving the server.

Me: it doesn't feel like a judgment-free zone anymore.

Tia: did you tell an admin?

Me: I didn't want to stir shit up. I hate confrontation.

Tia: lol I get that

Me: idk. I'll figure it out I guess.

Me: thanks for listening. I really appreciate it.

I cook dinner for the girls and myself. After we finish eating and clean up from dinner, I sit down on the couch to read on my Kindle. From the kids' room, I hear the opening tune to High School Musical, *Start of Something New*. Disney+ has been a hit in our house, and I'm stoked that the kids have 'discovered' some of my favorites. I toss my Kindle aside and dash into the girls' room, plopping down on the bed beside them. I sing along like a damn fool. Becca whines and tells me to stop while Callie giggles at my antics.

I may not be a Middle by some Kinksters' standards,

but I sure as fuck find comfort and joy in this space. Fuck the haters. You do you, I'm gonna do me.

19
"I HATE IT HERE"

SARAH

If I've said it once, I've said it a thousand times. I hate it here. It's the first day of school and the bus is already more than thirty minutes late. The bus tracking app isn't working, and there's no answer at the transportation office. The district didn't send out an email saying the bus was delayed. Nothing. So, here I am, standing outside in one-hundred-degree weather, full sun, and no shade while I wait at the bus stop. My pasty ass can't handle this shit. I could feel a burn forming on my skin within ten minutes of standing outside. Sarah and the outside do *not* get along. "I hate it here," I complain aloud.

Finally, the bus rolls up the street, yellow lights flashing. As the bus nears, the brakes squeal as it slows, red lights flash. The yellow monster halts, and the hydraulic brakes hiss. The driver opens the doors, they creak as they part. My girls barrel down the center aisle, grasping the handrail and hopping down the steps.

"Have a good one!" The driver waves as she reaches for the door handle, swinging the doors closed, and slowly pulling away from the bus stop to continue her route.

"How was your first day?" I ask, hugging each of my girls before we make the short trek back to the apartment.

"It was okay," Rebecca says.

"It was fun!"

"What did you do today?"

"Math!" Becca answers, suddenly excited.

"Math?" I match her enthusiasm. "And what about you, Callie?"

"I don't know. We learned stuff." She shrugs.

"Okay…Well, it was just the first day. I'm sure you'll learn a lot and have a lot of fun." We arrive back at the apartment. The girls feed the dogs and put on a show while I check their school folders for paperwork and announcements. There are already flyers for picture day. Two weeks from now. And a book fair pamphlet. *So, it begins.*

The girls and I have a nice, relaxing evening together. I cooked meatloaf which has become a favorite recently. Becca had seconds! Which is a miracle because I can hardly convince her to finish her dinner most nights. That's why I gave up on cooking shortly after Ryan left.

Callie and Rebecca get washed up before bed and clean their room. With the bus showing up before seven a.m., it's easier for them to shower at night. When they're ready for bed, they turn on a few episodes of Bluey. Just before bedtime, we call Ryan and the girls tell him all about their first day. The conversation doesn't last long since they don't have much to share about school. Callie tries to ask for a new video game, but we tell her we can discuss it later. It's bedtime now. We all tell Ryan 'Night, Night', and I climb into bed as well. It's been a long day for us all.

RYAN

INCOMING CALL: SARAH

"Hey, Babe," my voice croaks as I answer the phone. It's after eleven p.m. and I went to sleep almost three hours ago.

"They lost Rebecca," Sarah says. Her voice is strained, and shaky, yet somehow in control. "I'm going to find her."

"It's my fault," I hear Callie say. "They asked me what grade she's in. I said 'kinder' instead of 'pre-k'. I'm so stupid!"

"You're not stupid," Sarah tells her. "It's only the second day of school. You barely know your own teacher. How are you supposed to know hers? This is NOT your fault."

"What happened?" I ask, interrupting Sarah's frustrated lecture.

"They put her on the wrong fucking bus!"

"How the hell did that happen?"

"Fuck if I know! She was on the correct but yesterday! I gotta go. The school is calling me back. I'll call you when I know something. I love you."

"Love you." *Beep.* The call disconnects. *I guess I'm not sleeping tonight.*

SARAH

"You're asking me if I have an update?" I shout, not believing the bullshit I just heard through my car's Bluetooth.

"Yes, we were following up on your call," the secretary confirms.

"No, I don't have a fucking update. I wasn't the one who lost my fucking daughter! Someone is getting fired for this I swear to fucking God!" As I rage at the woman on the phone, another call from the school appears on my caller ID. "I gotta go. This is probably the principal." I hang up without waiting for her response.

"Hi, is this Rebecca Todd's mom?"

"Yes. Do you have an update on where she is?"

"We do not. We're working with the transportation office to find out which bus she was put on."

"School has been out for forty-five minutes and you still don't have accountability for my five-year-old daughter? This is fucking unacceptable!"

"Yes, ma'am, it is. I can't even imagine how you're feeling right now. You're welcome to come to the school and wait here while we call around for information."

"Oh, I'm already on the way there," I snap. "I'll be there in five minutes."

"Okay. We'll see you soon."

"Yep." I stab my thumb against the 'end call button on my steering wheel.

"They're going to find her, right, Mommy?" Callie sniffles from the backseat.

"Yeah, Honey. We're gonna find her." *God, please bring my baby home safe.*

Thirty more minutes on hold with the transportation office, awkward exchanges of pseudo-pleasantries with Becca's teacher, and so much pacing I've almost worn a hole in the carpet, we finally receive an update. I texted my boss that I'll be offline for the remainder of the day and likely tomorrow. I absolutely cannot handle anything else right now.

Rebecca strolls into the office as if nothing happened like she just went on a long bus ride. Meanwhile, we've all been freaking the fuck out. I take both daughters' hands, one hand in each of my own, and turn to leave. I give the principal a sharp nod and we leave. I'm done talking. I'm done with people. I want my kids, the couch, a huge blanket, and a Disney movie. *I fucking hate it here.*

It's been six weeks since the bus incident, and things haven't improved much. This school has no redeeming qualities, and I can't wait to move. They're not following Callie's Individualized Educational Plan, IEP, which is fucking illegal. She was diagnosed with ADHD last December and the ADHD is affecting her learning. The IEP is supposed to provide reasonable accommodations to ensure she meets her educational goals and help her succeed. *This stupid fucking school.*

On a positive note, Ryan got his next assignment. Another position opened on the list for his MOS. We're moving to California in December. He will be home in one more month. *Not that I'm counting or anything...* The downside to California is it's all the way across the country from family. Living in Oklahoma was already difficult because my family lives on the East Coast. It worked out when his parents moved from Wisconsin to be closer. In California, we won't have any support system in place. But it's okay. Ryan will be home. We will be together as a family again.

RYAN

"My flight is scheduled," I tell Sarah as she makes herself a cup of coffee. I watch her move in and out of view from the phone's camera as she busies herself throughout the cramped kitchen. "I'll be home on November 10th." That's only three weeks from now. We're in the final stretch.

"Yay!" She rushes back into view, a wide smile crossing her face. "I can't wait to see you."

"Have you worked on any packing to take in the vehicles for the drive out west?"

"Yes...I haven't just been sitting on my ass over here," she smarts.

"The movers will be there after I arrive. I asked my parents if we could stay with them for a few days before we take off. I figured it would be nice to spend Thanksgiving before we hit the road."

"Goody..." she rolls her eyes. "I'm not going to be able to work with the movers here."

"Work from my parents' house. Mom has her office she doesn't use."

"Fine. Make time move faster! I want you home already!" Sarah's face forms that adorable pout, the pout when she's fake-angry but cutesy and flirty.

"I'm gonna let you go, Babe. I'm gonna grab some dinner. I love you."

"I love you! MWAH!" She dramatically blows me a kiss and disconnects the call.

SARAH

Three weeks! He will be home in three weeks! I take a look around the tiny apartment and my mood sinks. I'm so ashamed of the state of this place. It's not dirty, I can't do dirty. But it's cluttered. There's stuff everywhere. We still have boxes we didn't unpack when we moved in a few months ago. We just replaced our couches, and the new ones are far too large for this temporary space. There is absolutely no fucking storage. *I hate it here.*

I make a plan to tackle one space at a time. Small chunks should make this less overwhelming, right? I consolidate a few things into one box, emptying another. I carry the empty box to the kids' room.

"Girls, I need you to be my super helpers, okay?"

"What are we doing?" Callie pulls her attention from the TV and climbs off the bed. Rebecca's eyes remain glued to the screen.

"I need you," I start, "Rebecca!" Her attention on me, I start again. "I need you to put what you want to take in the *car* in this box. Toys and stuffies, a few books. Stuff like that." I turn and walk the two steps to their closet to pull out their suitcases. "In the suitcases, put ten days of clothes. That means shirts, socks, underwear, pants, and pajamas."

"Okay."

"Now, what did I say?" If there's anything I've learned from having children, always instruct them to repeat what they were told to do. It helps reduce instances of miscommunication.

"Put the toys and stuff we want to take in the car in that box," Callie points.

"What else? Becca?"

"Pack the suitcases."

"With what?"

"Shirts, pants, pajamas, and underwear," Becca lists.

"And…?"

"Socks!" Callie grumbles.

"Yes. Ready? I'll check on you in thirty minutes. If you stay on task and finish up, maybe we can go bowling."

"Can we go to the place with the arcade and Laser tag?" Callie asks.

"Yeah! Laser tag!"

"Uh, yeah! I wanna play games too. But…only if you pack your stuff." An hour later, we're in the car driving to Oklahoma City to go bowling, play Laser tag, and live it up in the arcade.

20
IT'S HOMECOMING DAY!

SARAH

"Just a reminder, I'm taking off early today," I tell my coworkers during our mid-week meeting.

"Oh, that's right! Ryan's flying in today," my supervisor recalls. "I'm so glad your family will be reunited."

"Thank you. I'm just happy he's finally coming home. I really appreciate you all being flexible with me while he's been gone. I have no clue how single parents manage every day."

"You've been a valuable member of our team. We all have lives outside of work. Our jobs are never more important than family." My chin wrinkles and tears fill my eyes. I've never felt appreciated like this before, not at work. I take a few deep breaths before speaking. Thank God we don't use our cameras during out work calls. I'm a mess.

"Thank you. That means a lot. Really." After our emotional team bonding moment, we carry on business as usual.

Ryan is flying all day, so I won't hear from him until his connection in New York. I'm anxious, anticipation eats at me all day. I finally receive a message around one o'clock.

Ryan: landed in NY. Connection in less than 2 hours.
Me: is that enough time to clear customs and immigration?
Ryan: we're gonna find out

Since Ryan is back Stateside to stay, he has checked baggage. Flying internationally, he has to pick it up from baggage claim before going through customs, and then recheck the bags before going through TSA security again. *Fuck. Is he going to make it?!*

Ryan: on the plane. Grabbed a sandwich on the way. Fucking starving.
Me: omg I was freaking out!
Ryan: you're always freaking out
Me: ...
Ryan: lmao
Me: rude AF
Ryan: uh huh
Ryan: I gotta turn off my phone

Ryan: I love you A&F
Me: and I love you!

RYAN

I swear this has been one of the longest days of my fucking life. I was almost at a full-on sprint to the gate by the time I grabbed food. Now, my knee is killing me. There's a reason the Army gives us old, broken, assholes profiles. *Fuck.* There's a screaming baby on this flight, and the guy in front of me has his seat all the way back. The already tight space feels even tighter. I'm not claustrophobic, but this is making me overwhelmed for sure.

It's a few hours to Dallas and a transfer to the regional airport in Oklahoma. I text Sarah when the flight lands in Dallas. I walk to the next departure gate and attempt to decompress a bit, putting in my earbuds and scrolling Tiktok videos on my phone.

"Good afternoon. We're ready to start boarding Flight 121 to Oklahoma-Fort Regional Airport." I remove my earbuds and pack them away. I text Sarah letting her know the flight is starting to board and I should be there soon.

Sarah: I can't wait!
Sarah: see you soon!
Sarah: have a safe flight! I love you!!!!!!!
Me: and I love you! A&F.

"Active duty service members and passengers with small children, welcome aboard." I make my way to the door, the gate agent scans my ticket. "Enjoy your flight."

"Thanks." I cross the threshold and walk down the hall of the creaky sky ramp. I step onto the plane and maneuver through the cramped aisle to find my seat. I retrieve my earbuds from my backpack before stowing my gear and sitting down. *Almost there.*

SARAH

Ryan: flight just touched down.
Me: yay! Leaving now!

Since the apartment is only a few minutes away from the airport, it makes more sense to leave now. I can't wait at the pick up/drop off lane too long, and it's silly to pay for parking for ten minutes. He should be finished at baggage claim by the time we get there. Perfect timing.

"Girls! Let's go!"

"Where are we going?" Becca asks.

"Airport," I answer as I latch the dogs' crate.

"Dad's coming home?" Callie's voice is hopeful and excited.

"Yep! Now, let's go!" Not needing to be told again, the girls run outside, and I lock up. I take long strides to catch up, and the kids are waiting not-so-patiently beside my car. I press the button on the remote to unlock the doors and they climb in. I buckle Rebecca into her seat and slide into the driver's seat. *Off we go.*

As I turn into the airport's arrivals and departures lane, I'm glad to see there aren't many vehicles in line waiting. I'm able to pull over rather than circle the small airport parking or pay to park. Within five minutes, people start to emerge from the sliding automatic doors. I see Ryan step outside, so I press the button to open the back of the car, the door rising slowly as he walks toward the car. I climb out to meet him, a smile crosses my face and happy tears fill my eyes. *He's finally home!*

"Hey, Babe," he props his wheelie suitcases, so they won't roll away, and holds his arms open. I step into his embrace and hold him tight.

"You're not allowed to leave again," I sniffle into his chest. I pull back slightly and look at him in his handsome face. "Ima fight them if they take you away again." He laughs a little at my threat.

"Pretty sure it doesn't work like that." Ryan leans in and kisses me deeply. "I missed you, Babe," He says, breaking our kiss.

"I missed you, too."

"Dad!" Callie yells, turning around in her seat. "We missed you, too!"

"Yeah!" Becca agrees.

"Ready to see the apartment?" I ask, wincing.

"Let's go." Ryan kisses the top of my head and walks to the passenger side of the car.

Back at the apartment, I order us pizza. We'd rather spend the evening together than in the kitchen, and Ryan didn't want to go out anywhere. *Yes, I cook!* The dogs immediately want all the love from the man. *Traitors.* And the kids have to show Ryan all the things.

"Look, Dad! Do you like my Lego robot?" Becca proudly holds up her Lego creation.

"That's awesome."

"I drawed this picture," Callie hands Ryan a picture of an Imposter from Among Us. *I think that's what she called them...*

"'Drew'," I remind her.

"I drew this picture," she corrects herself.

"Wow! This is great," Ryan tells her. She smiles.

"I have a lot more!"

"We can show Daddy later. Let's relax for now. I'm sure he's had a very long day of traveling."

We have a nice, relaxing family evening with a Disney movie and microwave popcorn. The kids chose Toy Story tonight. We haven't watched it in a while so it's a nice change. I'm glad it's not Bruno anymore.

He's finally home.

EPILOGUE
IS IT AN EPILOGUE IF IT'S A TRUE STORY AND WE'RE STILL LIVING IT?

One Year Later

SARAH

Ryan moved back to the States one year ago. We stayed at his parents' house for about a week which went surprisingly well. His mom cried when we left, as usual. We then drove four-fucking-days across the country to California.

California has been pretty nice so far. The kids love their school, and Ryan loves his new unit. The soldiers give him shit for being 'old' because he's in his mid-30s. He's officially old enough to be these kids' father!

Our marriage is great, but the Dom/sub dynamic is pretty much non-existent. Ryan encourages my Middle stuff but he's not really 'Daddy', and that's okay. Sometimes if I'm feeling especially Middle-y, I'll still call him 'Daddy'. He is super supportive, and that's amazing. He buys me stuffies, kitty ears, and other Middle-y goodies and presents. After a long day, he will pick one of my favorite movies to help me get into a better headspace. The man voluntarily put on The Princess Diaries! And snackies. He gets me all the snackies! On date nights, we'll do grown-up stuff sometimes, but he finds Middle activities I enjoy. We went bowling a few weeks ago. It was so fun to be carefree and the bowling alley had music from my teen years on the stereo. It was awesome.

We still have kinky sex sometimes with the leather smackie, smackies, bondage, and other toys. We tried a little Shabari a while back. I think my anxiety can't handle it. I don't like feeling stuck, even with safety shears nearby. Sometimes he calls me filthy names in bed, then he tells me I'm a Good Girl and how much he loves me. It's a balance.

Even with all we've learned and experimented with, vanilla is pretty standard. I have no idea how 24/7 dynamic couples with kids have kinky sex on the regular anyway. That shit takes time to set up and it's not exactly quiet. Rebecca already heard us having sex before (vanilla), and banged on the door asking 'Mommy, are you okay? Mommy?' I can't even imagine what the kids would think if they heard swooshes, swats, and snaps of leather against skin.

It's been a journey, and it's still going. We've been together for a decade. We've grown as individuals and as a couple, but we've also changed. Every day we learn more about ourselves and about each other. We work on ourselves every day. We work on our marriage every day. No, we're not perfect, but we work through our differences because we love each other. He's my person. I'll stand by his side and follow him anywhere.

NOTE FROM THE AUTHOR

Thank you so much for reading! This is based on the true story of my husband and myself. I wanted to write a book to show the real struggles of military families. Throughout our separation, I gained some amazing friends and learned more about myself. That's why this book is part of my Dirty Doms series.

I was hesitant to publish this book. I have been terrified of reader criticism and negative feedback for this book specifically. It took a lot of vulnerability to write, and with every reader, I open myself up to more criticism. But with every reader, I also have the opportunity to make others feel seen. I think we all want to feel like we belong and know that we're not alone. I want my books to be relatable, and I hope I captured that.

If you enjoyed this book, please leave a rating/review. I'd love to know what you think. If you have feedback, please reach out directly. K.cartyauthor@gmail.com

ABOUT THE AUTHOR

K. Carty is an Armed Forces veteran and military spouse. She enjoys Disney movies and shows, anime, video games, and reading smut.

Don't forget to follow me on social media!
IG: https://www.instagram.com/k.cartyromance/
Tiktok: https://www.tiktok.com/@k.cartyauthor
Website: https://kcartyauthor.wixsite.com/kcarty

Made in the USA
Monee, IL
28 April 2024